AFTER THE SUNDIAL

Vera Nazarian

Cover Art:
"After the Sundial," Copyright © 2010 by Vera Nazarian
Image Elements: "Star Cluster Bursts Out" by NASA, J. Trauger (JPL), J. Westphal (Caltech); "The Life of Stars" by Wolfgang Brandner, Eva K. Grebel You-Hua Chu (NASA), March 5, 1999; "Sun-dial on the south-wall of the monastery of Gurk, Carinthia, Austria," photo by Johann Jaritz, November 26, 2006; "Sundial" clip art, public domain image, wpclipart.com

Cover Design Copyright © 2010 by Vera Nazarian

ISBN-13: 978-1-60762-077-8
ISBN-10: 1-60762-077-4

Trade Paperback Edition

August 20, 2010

A Publication of
Norilana Books
P. O. Box 2188
Winnetka, CA 91396
www.norilana.com

Printed in the United States of America

After the Sundial

Norilana Books
Science Fiction

www.norilana.com

Other Books by Vera Nazarian

Dreams of the Compass Rose
Lords of Rainbow
The Clock King and the Queen of the Hourglass
Mayhem at Grant-Williams High (YA)
The Duke in His Castle
Salt of the Air
Mansfield Park and Mummies

AFTER the
SUNDIAL

Vera Nazarian

Contents:

INTRODUCTION

by Vera Nazarian

I am primarily considered to be a writer of myth and fantasy. For the most part it's true, but over the years I've written a fair amount of science fiction of various degrees of "rigor" or squishiness—enough in fact for a collection.

Admittedly, science fiction does not come as naturally to stir my imagination factory as fantasy. But when challenged, I am happy to take my ethereal wonder dreams into the far reaches of space-time and the "what if?" territory of shiny high-tech and scientific speculation.

One thing you may not know: I've been a hardware computer tech for several decades, and my various tech support day jobs have marked me irrevocably as a *nerd*. Notice, I don't say *geek*—a geek is the cool, trendy, tech-savvy person, a term basically synonymous these days with a highly proficient and skilled professional and modern intellectual, a mover and shaker of our age. A nerd, on the other hand, is the not-so-cool version of the technical person, someone who is often relegated to the back of the back room, someone not particularly aware or interested in whether they are wearing a dingy stained shirt *inside-out* and their socks don't match their pants (or even each other . . . wait, what pants?).

A geek might decorate their cube with snappy geek memorabilia (Dilbert cartoon clips, Comdex freebies and oh-so prestigious Exhibitor badges of trade show glories past) and necessarily use high-end Apple products. A nerd is invariably a PC user and lives in the cube like they would in their bedroom (what decoration?), makes little social contact beyond the cubicle wall or the break room microwave, and quotes tech manuals, HEX codes, and *The Hitchhiker's Guide to the Galaxy* interchangeably at inappropriate moments.

In fact, the key word is "inappropriate." Geeks know and care what it means, nerds don't. The distinction is short and sweet.

Okay, here are more differences, for a more subtle appreciation. In general, a modern geek knows the practical advantages of science, has well-defined goals, and always keeps one eye on the big picture, while the nerd just basks in the details and the process and enjoys the ride. A geek waxes eloquent about latest generation microprocessors and what they can *do* for her or him, while a nerd waxes eloquent about jumper settings and what they can *do* in the on and off position, period—see what I'm getting at here? A nerd can barely talk to marketing, while a geek can do their own marketing. It's all in the perspective, in what's important. And in whether or not you care.

A fine example of a fabulous female geek is Penelope Garcia from *Criminal Minds*. And female nerds are . . . well, me. Well, okay, on a good day I can be a geek with the best of them. Sometimes. But it's not my natural state, because I am too much of a slob, and it takes more effort to do "geek" properly.

So, what does that have to do with science fiction?

Well, you might say that for all these years I've had a series of day jobs that have been pretty much science fiction. I've huddled in small, claustrophobic, strongly air-conditioned server closets humming with cooling fans and filled with tiny blinking drive lights (and before that, mainframe rooms) that could have been shipboard crew quarters on board the *Battlestar Galactica.* I've jumped rope with lengths of discarded network cable during breaks; played ping pong matches with fellow nerdo-geek co-workers in narrow warehouse aisles between stacks of circuit boards and soldering material. . . .

I've eaten lunch surrounded by multiple monitors, consoles, gaping CPU carcasses, gutted printers and other machinery body parts straight out of *The Terminator;* spent 8:00 AM to 6:00 PM (and in later years, the soothing night shift) attached with more wires than one can image to more telephony—headsets, handsets, clip-ons, RF wireless, walkie talkie, satellite hookup, and other phone system variations (long before there was such a thing as Bluetooth)—than a Borg from *Star Trek* (fun factoid: I've even lived in the actual real-life Borg—the dorm in my *alma mater* Pomona College upon which the *Star Trek* alien race "the Borg" were based). For that matter, I've programmed phone system diagnostic logic engines (that universally annoying software that makes response decisions based on the buttons you press on your touch-tone phone), so that sometimes it felt like I was painfully communicating with a less homicidal version of HAL 9000 from *2001: A Space Odyssey.*

I've taken emergency or "life and death" tech support calls and helped thousands of screaming people install their printer drivers, diagnose paper out sensor problems, create barcodes on deadline, while simultaneously playing *Doom, Heretic, Descent, Wolfenstein, Tetris, Monuments of Mars, Nibbles* (the DOS 5 "worm" game—literally, not in the virus sense), and feeling like Ellen Ripley in the heat of an *Aliens* gun battle, besieged from all directions, locations, dimensions, and area codes. . . . Ah, the good old days. Such fun, but now I have technology burnout and carpal tunnel. (Good thing I stayed away from early *World of Warcraft,* or I'd really be in trouble!)

And now that I have a choice in the matter (not about carpal tunnel, of course, but that I am self-employed), I don't even own a cell phone.

So maybe that's kind of why I normally dream and write fantasy as opposed to science fiction—the SF is just ordinary real life.

But when the right elements combine in the imagination and it really *is* time to write SF, it's a great feeling when a science fiction idea (and then the story stemming from the idea) comes together. And I am proud to consider myself a science fiction writer as much as I am a writer of anything else.

What a strange thing it is, this thing called genre. Mystery, romance, fantasy, science fiction, thriller, literary—what the heck are they, when each can incorporate heavy elements of the others?

Is it all just arbitrary marketing decisions and product placement, or is it something else? In this particular moment I'd say, genre is somewhat like the rainbow, a true gradual continuum of degree, from one color to the other, as opposed to discrete units. Or, if you prefer a science metaphor, genre is not a particle but a wave. And yet—depending on what aspect you choose to focus, there you have it. Ask me again and I might have a different answer. How very quantum of me.

Genre is merely a conscious choice. Once you decide that the color you are seeing is orange as opposed to dark peachy yellow, you've made a genre classification decision.

Maybe such ambiguity of definition is why the differences between fantasy and science fiction have always been the stuff of contention, confusion, and often randomness. Some things feel more like fantasy, others like science fiction. And who is to say they are not?

My criteria and definition of science fiction is a bit more concrete. The stories I decided to include here are the ones I feel *could* happen in our physical universe, no matter how outlandish. And that includes speculation about the mysteries and unexplored aspects of *time*.

Time is the overlying theme in all these stories. Not necessarily time travel but time in its raw nature, the ephemerality, the breaks and the continuity, the strange ways of measuring or experiencing it. The mystique of time as a continuum (again, like the rainbow) along which we experience events. Our own places in time as temporal markers of sorts, Particles in a stream of one great Wave.

In addition to stories, I've included a couple of poems which I feel belong. (Not that I am much of a poet—I don't ever consider myself one, even though I write poetic prose). But occasionally poems happen to me.

Some of the highlights here: the very first poem (or written work of any kind) of mine that has seen print—I wrote "What is Time?" in 9th or 10th grade, and had it "published" in what I then did not know was a vanity book for which I (my parents) paid over thirty bucks (being a kid, I did not know the difference between professional publication versus self-published or any other kind). Another is "Port Custodial Blues," a WSFA Small Press Award 2007 Finalist.

There are two previously unpublished pieces here, the poem "Scent of the Stars" written after my father's death in 2008, and short story "Salmon in the Drain Pipe" written a while ago, but revised now, inspired by the tragic events of the BP oil spill disaster in the Gulf of Mexico.

The last piece is a long novella, or short novel, *The Clock King and the Queen of the Hourglass,* originally published in book form in the UK by PS Publishing, with an introduction by Charles de Lint. It made the 2005 Locus Recommended Reading List, received a *Year's Best* Honorable Mention from Gardner Dozois, garnered good reviews and other critical acclaim.

How curious or prophetic is any of it? I leave it for you to consider.

Take your time.

WHAT IS TIME?

he question was asked before the dawn of time.

Time went by and they built sundials in the sand of Egypt.

When the sun set, they slumbered and dreamed of yesterday.

In the morning Rome rose, flourished, and fell,
Like the yellow sand of an hourglass.

One more hour, and the sacred hordes overran the East,
Calling it Crusades.

And in three minutes they split the first atom over a city,
Without considering tomorrow.

A meager second was enough to venture into space,
While the Milky Way hung in the sky
Like a trail of white sand and dust.

Now they look back, asking the question
Raised before the dawn of time . . .

They still have their sand.

THE BALLAD OF UNIVERSAL JACK

In the beginning was the word. At first, it meant jack. But then it issued past lips and out of a cosmic mouth. That changed it. It was now loaded. It formed semantic ripples in the fabric of the dark matter around it, and became a pattern. The pattern stretched itself into an immeasurable span of radiance, and became the universe.

Much later, another, lesser mouth opened—a mouth of carbon-based organic flesh and water—and out came human language.

"So, why are you telling me this?" said Reanne. "Is it because I am supposed to open my lips and utter pearls for your swine ears?"

She was speaking to herself, of course, looking in the mirror. There was no sound, since she made no actual effort to vocalize, but her lips moved lightly, folds of soft rose flesh, and steam coagulated on the glass surface.

Her self answered with more esoteric thoughts and nonsense syllables, and a long discourse ensued in the span of a millisecond—Reanne and the other *deeper* Reanne—upon the nature of pearls and swine, while Reanne dried her long dark clumps of soggy hair, and then wrapped herself in old terrycloth.

She then stepped outside beyond the steam, where Matt waited for her, and she let the robe fall open, so that he could see her, while she also could see him, that part of him, rising. Matt sat on the bedcovers, leaning back, and she came forward, and put her albedo-white hands on his dark-side-of-the-moon-dark shoulders, leaned into him full force.

She positioned herself just above him, and took a dancer's stance, loose at the knees, and then engulfed him with her vagina, sinking into impalement, sliding loose and soft and inevitable like a snowflake against a lamppost, in the dark grim winter.

His lips muttered something, words issued out of him, and he moved beneath her, spanning her with the pattern of radiance, and he became immeasurable.

She sank and rose and fell, and words came spurting in her mind, words and litanies and forms of lace.

When it was all over—or rather, the rest of things commenced—Reanne disengaged herself, and lay back on the bedcovers, and stared up into the ceiling. She felt the moisture, the semantic load of waters cooling at her thighs.

While in her mind, her other self continued uttering words upon words of esoteric wisdom that had no beginning and no end, no relevance to her, and hence meant nothing and would not yield their cargo.

A little while later, or maybe a lot, Reanne—now an old withered creature—lay in a place of whiteness and sterility, while two young women and a boy stared down at her fading self. The boy was a grandchild, and one of the women was her daughter, and the direct issue of that encounter in a room of pale steam. The other woman was the daughter's geno-clone, and the boy's real mother. Or, at least she had been there when the boy cried, and when he needed someone to confess his sin dreams—certainly not the innermost ones, but those floating like cream upon the surface, those that could be disclosed without involvement.

The geno-clone was perfect, because when she spoke, her lips hardly moved at all, so that it seemed the words came forth out of the air itself, were thrown by a ventriloquist. In fact, the geno-clone spoke very little at all, and listened, and let the boy talk mostly, let him move his mouth rapidly and passionately in the throes of young speech, swallowing all logic and most of the meaning.

Reanne's daughter, Mariah, was speaking now. She was sobbing, her lips quivering, swollen nose, discolored brimming eyes. The issuing wetness made patterns upon her cheeks. Occasional drops came to fall upon Reanne's bed coverings. Mariah's geno-clone stood silent, holding the boy with her hands, and absently stroking his forehead.

Reanne's own dry lips moved once with the effort of trying to say something, until Mariah motioned for a nurse to bring a device that would temporarily give Reanne the ability to speak, despite her destroyed lungs.

The nurse attached the expensive device to Reanne's life support, and suddenly the room echoed with a strong voice of the old woman, issuing out of the air and the walls. The boy, standing all this time with his lids closed, opened his eyes and started to listen, for it reminded him so much of the geno-clone's aerial manner of speaking—safe, familiar, and *real*.

"What do you all want?" said Reanne. "I want you to know that I have nothing to say. Nothing new, except that you are all swine, and I am casting pearls before you, and yet I love you as I love salt."

"Mother?" sobbed Mariah. "What do you mean, mother?"

"Like I said, swine," said the old woman, and then motioned with her finger. "Take this thing away."

And then she was silent, and closed her eyes, and wouldn't speak again. They disconnected the device finally, since every moment was costing Mariah immeasurable credits.

A bit later, the old woman died.

The boy watched his grandmother, her final passing unmarked, and something started in his mind, words and syllables, and song, and his lips began to move, while the geno-clone continued to gently stroke his hair.

The boy blinked, and he was a man. His mother—or was it the geno-clone; he could never keep them straight any longer, ever since he decided to stop needing to feel maternal warmth—his mother was an old woman herself, and he hardly went to see either one of them.

Instead, the man was tall and strong, and he worked with large machines in a brightly lit room, wearing a protective full-body suit of fine plastic-metal alloy. The room was not a room exactly, but the loading dock of a space station, high above the earth's surface, and nearer in fact to the moon's orbit.

In space, except for the radio-transmitted holo-vocals, there were hardly any words, only silence. All earth speech was delayed by the cosmic distances, and communication was a matter of gestures or light codes that would show up on the receiver panels of his suit at both his wrists.

When the man was done with his work shift, he would enter the inner dock, and then the low-gravity outer ring of the station. Here, he turned in his heavy gear and became just Jack Westrig. It was the name he had earned with his own efforts. The previous Jack Westrig had been exceptionally creative and hard to live up to. All of the Jacks had been like that, swift, logical, full of formative energy. It took an extraordinary man to become Jack.

This Jack Westrig had a secret. When he took off his work gear, he also put on an alternate frame of mind which included an acute verbal sense of beauty. Jack was a poet, because he would walk through corridors of the station and words would tumble into his mind out of the air, from the walls of metal alloy.

Maybe these words came in like neutrino particles through the hull, through the walls, and simply entered him, being ancient messengers of distant galaxies, carrying with them primeval seeds of the subatomic birth of stars? Or maybe they were white noise in his cortex.

Jack's mind seethed, bouncing raw crystal and rubber images, dissonant in their own internal dichotomy, and forming into fractal patterns of perfect imperfection. Jack had secretly learned dozens of human earth languages, and he would mouth the roots of words, feel their shape, and then use combinations of those linguistic roots to describe new terms, new words from the alien forms that came to him from the stars.

In his room, a woman greeted Jack. She was young and full-bodied, and he had felt sexually and emotionally drawn to her for some time now, seeing her in the botanosphere of the station, but had been unable to approach her.

But because his need had been so great, he had written her through the net.

And apparently the poetic idiocy of his confession rendered in electrons had had their desired effect, for here she was, whether out of curiosity, or pity, or perversity, he was not sure. Did it matter?

She smiled at him, and came forward, and he saw that she had drawn the throat of her suit open all the way to her waist, and inside she wore nothing else. Her body came bursting through, mauve nipples sharp like flower buds on great round animal whiteness. . . .

He took hold of her, moving in reflex, and drew her close, while sine waves of disconnected words and word roots began to race through his mind. After several moments of fumbling movement, intimate tactile exploration, and alien wilderness, she suddenly pushed him away.

"You're just like all the rest of them, Jack," she said, wiping her lips, breathing fast, and her breasts quivering while she stuffed them hurriedly back inside her outfit. "I thought you'd be different, with your pretty images and fractal thoughts, and your need for me."

"What?" he said in confusion, rendered verbally impotent by this unexpected turn.

"Just like a man. Now you have nothing to say to me. You are a pig, Jack," said the nameless woman. "And I don't need to cast my pearls before you."

"But . . ." he again started, unbelieving. "But you—"

You must love me like salt, he wanted to end.

She made him lose his pattern of words. Her accusation made no sense. She came to him, offered herself, and now this? And she expected him to understand what she had anticipated from him in return? The encounter degenerated into a reminder that there were no means to bridge the cosmic comprehension void between male and female.

It was a wonder the species persisted, extended into the cosmic vacuum beyond earth. All these languages, nuances, and still no common ground, except through a blurred filter of demonstrated intent followed by feedback reinforcement. No common definitions for words and terms that seemed to be clone-similar yet obviously had to be residing in interlaced but separate dimensions.

The problem arose within Jack's mind, and in that instant he forgot the rejection, so taken was he with a creative possibility.

"Not just a pig, but a distracted idiot," said the woman, as she left his room, while the door slid softly in her wake.

Unlike the door with its functional motion sensors, he didn't even notice her leaving, because in that moment words came alive in a drift of snowflakes, and were swirling in his mind.

In the following weeks, Jack Westrig hummed a tune as he worked with the great mechanical monsters in the vacuum of the loading dock. He was doing the most delicate work of bio-electric repair on the machines, yet for some reason his poetry would not leave him as it normally did during his work shift.

A white sun-lit space bird came sailing into the dock in perfect cosmic silence, a ship from the outer solar system. He stared, watching its brilliant albedo against the vacuum of space in the background, and saw it as one great big Word.

We send parts of ourselves, these Words, forth into the outer space around us. They represent us as a species, they speak for us to anyone and anything that might be out there, waiting.

And yet, why couldn't humanity communicate perfectly within itself? Why was there a gap between sexes, and ages and blood-bonds and generations, even between the self of childhood and adulthood?

How could it then expect to reach out into the greater universe and make any damn sense?

Thoughts and words and acts are not enough. Not enough to demonstrate one's love of salt by casting pearls before swine.

The moment passed and Jack continued his delicate techno-surgery, while a resolution was forming inside him. In hours, days, weeks, it would flower and bear fruit.

Jack was certain he had made a theoretical discovery of post-quantum linguo-physics, an absurdly easy missing link— not so much missing as misplaced. And he presented a part of it to a committee of the top scientists on the station.

Jack stood and spoke, and as images entered him together with the oxygen, language poured out of him with the exhaled carbon dioxide, and shaped his breath and solidified into water vapor. While, inside him, the essence of salt remained.

The panel listened, and one scientist, Miro Wastman, nodded slowly, and then stood up, and reached with his hand forward, palm upturned, and stood waiting for Jack to react to his hand.

"I know what you want me to do," said Jack, refusing to complete the handshake. "But I will not do it, just to demonstrate that my theory is valid."

"You're merely stalling and embellishing," said Miro.

Jack smiled. "Not at all. I am merely creating the future."

And so it was.

In the next earth year, the Westrig Theory of Formation was officially recorded in the annals of scientific knowledge, where it was promptly filed away and forgotten, as happens to all things most basic and as old as the species—things of naïveté or disguised subtlety.

The idea that words created the universe.

Jack Westrig had argued that by organizing sensory incoming information into humanly recognizable patterns—thought—and then by externalizing those patterns into a symbolic form called language, human beings were able to perform actions based upon those thoughts. And sequences of actions formed the future.

And not just *homo sapiens*, Jack had said, but any other form of sentience did this. We merely conceive something, and then take steps to make it happen—tomorrow, the next year, or in the next millennium. Every single thing now is the result of someone's word.

And notice, I do not say *thought*, but *word*. Why? Because a thought is private and internal, left to echo emptily against the inner boundaries of the mind. But a word—in its broadest meaning, an external symbol—is the first outward communication of one's intent.

Also, I say a word, and not an action, Jack continued. Action is merely the interpretation. It is the going through the motions of one's intent without communicating it to others. It can and will be misconstrued, and will fall like a seed onto barren soil to be left to its own devices. But only an action directly accompanied by a word is going to cross the bridge between now and the future. Because it will be a thing shared, and hopefully understood—a goal given form and meaning.

We open our lips and define the immediate shape that the universe takes around us, whether we offer—or withhold—a hand in greeting, or a ship into the cosmic void.

And saying that, Jack died. Because he'd been saying it for the last fifty earth years, and Jack Westrig had now become an old man.

But his word lived on beyond his life span, and into the future. It was a minor commonsense thing, a forgettable theory, and yet it was the only and best offspring he had left. For the word shaped not only his future but that of others, as one day they will venture into the farthest reaches by means of tools they themselves conceived in the distant past of today.

Indeed, words are the best offspring. They are the catalyst cause, with all else the effect. Even now, words from the distant past originated by *someone*, race on ahead, and slip deviously through us, through past, present, and future, ending universes, and beginning new ones. In many cases they have devolved into proverbial clichés, but, Jack would tell you, never underestimate them.

Now, Jack is immortal. His DNA is dissolved into the universal soup but his little word has gone on ahead of him forever, spreading creative tentacles of meaning forward, hurtling through the nothingness between the stars.

If you miss a blink, you might even catch the word and hitch a circular ride on it that will swing you all the way to the beginning, and back again here, to the end.

You may even be doing it now, reading this.

Or, maybe not; there is more to the nature of words than simple meaning. Meaning is a charge, a positive load; not a constant but a constant process.

And yet—as all immortals, Jack is a joker. He is like his grandmother, and the ones who came before them, in his love of salt and—unlike others—in his knowledge of its true value.

As all jokers, Jack is also wary of confessing what is innermost, and has only given us the cream off the top. He has learned not to cast all his cliché pearls before swine, holding back just enough.

Jack may speak the word, and may even *be* the word. But a word alone is nothing, and means jack. And even together, thoughts and words and acts and intentions are not enough.

In the beginning came the positive charge of original definition.

A TIME TO CRAWL

The old man got down on all fours and began to Crawl. This time he had lasted upright almost seventy feet from the entrance to the apartment building before his juices ran out and he had to do it. That was about twenty to fifteen feet less than yesterday.

He wasn't counting, of course. Just watching for landmarks. For example, he'd gotten past that gray dumpster ahead, and had made it nearly to the tree on the corner, only a block and a half away from the bus stop.

His knee-pads were good strong rayon, probably the best he could buy for twenty dollars. He'd mail-ordered them from an online catalog at Work two weeks ago, to replace the old worn-out sets that had lasted him almost six months. And the new set had arrived just in time, together with the reinforced workman gloves and elbow-pads. Just in time to boost him, now that he was actually showing the first signs of daily difficulty.

Actually it's been over ten months that he'd been Crawling. Sandra had seen it coming way before he had, just as she had known she'd be bedridden starting last spring. It was in the stoop of his back, she'd said, in the asthmatic short breath every time he'd make it up the stairs, and the fact that his lower legs were stiff and numb every night, and she had to rub them back to life for half an hour before sleep.

Of course, everyone's symptoms were different. Everyone had different medical reasons for Crawling. And after all, he was seventy-six, a time when over 60 percent of the population started to Crawl. Many people started as young as sixty. And Sandra never even Crawled at all; she just skipped it altogether to become permanently confined to a bed.

"Hey, Crawler, watch it!" someone said. The old man continued Crawling without turning his head, but edged closer to the rightmost edge of the sidewalk. He knew better than to get in the way of Walkers, or those occasional Paddlers.

Paddlers were Crawlers that had somehow adapted skateboards to fit knee-pads, and rolled to the bus stop. Paddlers were dangerous, often losing control of the boards and rolling into traffic and ending up in accidents, so that not many lasted. He knew what risks it involved, but he often envied them nevertheless, envied their much-improved ease of movement.

And then there were the fortunate few, the elite Wheelers. They had been the ones whose families had received fed or state wheelchairs before the Senior Reform Act, the complete abolition of fed and state welfare aid in the past century. Or they had been lucky enough to have enough money to pay for their own. Wheelchairs had been family heirlooms handed down to the children, especially since the post Senior Reform amendments also denied driver licenses to those over fifty-five.

The old man paused at the end of the block, near the tree, and lay down on his stomach to rest, taking deep breaths that sucked in air. His temples pounded from the strain, and his chest hurt acutely.

"Morning, Nelson," said the old woman who was lying at the tree, gasping heavily, and forcing a thin smile on her withered lips. Her cap had come askew, and her heavy gloves, sweats and knee-pads were covered with soggy dew-soaked street grime.

"Morning, Jane," he replied, after catching his breath, and then thought of asking how she was, and how was the family and

Richard, but decided that would be too much energy wasted. So, he simply nodded, then lay down with his cheek in the dirt. He closed his eyes.

As if she had read his mind, the old woman also turned back and ignored him. Then, a couple of minutes later, she glanced at her watch, and then with lots of weak infirm moans and other noise, gathered herself up and began to Crawl, past him, onto the curb. There, she pressed the Crawler floor-level pedestrian button on the floor of the post that controlled traffic signals. Having requested the extended Crawler "Walk" signal, she remained on her knees, poised for movement like a panting dog, as she waited for the light to change.

The old man got up on his elbows, and looked at his own watch. Six-thirty-three.

He had exactly twenty-seven minutes to make it to the bus stop to catch the seven am bus. The seven-fifteen was too late. It would make him late for his eight am shift. The bus arrived downtown at seven-forty-five, and he needed at least fifteen minutes to Crawl to the building, to make it to the sixth floor elevator, and to finally Plug himself In. . . . He'd measured it precisely within one or two minutes difference.

And he had to clock in exactly at eight to get the full credit for the whole day's Work shift, On-Time Status, and no later than eight-oh-five to get Near-On-Time.

And today, of all days, he had to make On-Time to get the full two-week paycheck for the month. Today was the one day he woke up late, couldn't get himself out of bed. Such a simple thing, and yet, it was harder and harder to get out of bed every morning. Besides, a chronic insomniac, he could never get up on time, not even back when he was young and had the energy.

He just couldn't.

And today—today, that paycheck was going to take care of the big bill, the one for Sandra. . . .

Thinking of Sandra, he heaved a great lungful, cursing himself in his mind, and lifted himself on his knees, automatically adjusting his right elbow pad that was always shifting a little.

And then he began to Crawl forward.

He got to the curb just as the light had changed. Jane had already Crawled across the short four-lane street, and was on the distant other block sidewalk. He could see the slow regular movements of her thin buttocks encased in those dark loose sweats, her shriveled thin legs dragging behind her like dead weights. Jane had been Crawling only about five months now, and was still in that halfway stage where she was strong in the sense of being new at it, still almost a Walker, and yet weak from lack of practice. But she was learning fast enough.

"Watch it, Crawler! Keep to your right!"

Again, he heard some Walker grumble at him, and rather than seeing the shadow of feet, heard the sound of quickly racing heels against pavement. Walkers often sped past him at this time every morning, nearly at a run, trying to catch that bus. He remembered well, because only ten months ago he had been one of them, had shuffled quickly past others with already severely hurting feet, holding on to the two walking canes in both his hands, like ski-poles. . . .

He depressed the Crawler signal button, and remained on his knees, putting his full weight forward on his strong toned arms, watching the sea of cross traffic at tire level.

Big truck wheels, smaller passenger car tires, shiny chrome hubcaps, dirty rubber and grease and grime-covered old hubcaps, wide rubber tires with brand names in painted relief, worn in treads, new coarse huge treads. . . .

All, spinning.

He noted small ovoid imperfections in their spinning as they flew by, watched the missing nuts and screws on some, the caps over the air plugs, the scratches. . . .

The light turned green. The spinning ovoids slowed as the vehicles braked, and he momentarily stared at the way they rolled into place and sat there motionless, exhaust pipes puffing gray poison smoke, just feet away, right into his face.

He started moving down the curb onto the street, just as the wind brought a gust of the carbon monoxide right into his lungs.

Next to him, a surge of feet, as Walkers bounded forward, racing to cross the street. Next to him, and behind him, nearly single file, came the Crawlers, forming a single human chain of slower, and yet remarkably fast movement.

Right hand forward, left hand forward. . . . Drag right knee (and with it the dead weight of leg), drag left knee. . . .

He was almost across the street now, following the wide painted white stripes on the walkway, counting them, twenty exactly. He had reached number seventeen.

Someone accidentally pushed against his left foot from behind.

He ignored it, and continued counting stripes, eighteen, nineteen, twenty, and was at the curb.

This was the hard part. He put both his hands on the curb, then grunted, and brought the rest of himself by sheer force of arms, to lie on the new sidewalk. And only then, after a second of in-drawn breath, he straightened, and again raised himself on his knees.

As always, there was some pushing and a fumble behind him, as the next Crawler in line behind him had gotten to the curb, and had to make that extra effort to raise oneself.

But Nelson was already several feet ahead, beginning the long uninterrupted stretch of the final block. Unfortunately this city block went on forever, past the large schoolground that was a sea of concrete and chain-link fencing, and then the shopping center. At the very end, about fifty feet from the corner of a busy intersection, stood the coveted bus stop—a large tented structure that would accommodate up to fifty people and provide overhead shelter from unfavorable weather to at least thirty.

They would pack it like sardines.

Crawlers and Paddlers would be allowed to take up the marked yellow floor space to the right, against one of the walls of the overhang. During bad weather, some would fight for the places nearest the wall. But their one undeniable advantage was that they were allowed to board the bus first—it was the only guarantee they had.

Two thirds of remaining space would be taken up by the Walkers who stood jam-packed together like vertical canned sausages, primed for pentathlon sprint action as soon as the bus appeared and the two sets of doors opened. They stood, hearts pumping, adrenaline filling their systems, ready to make a crazed push forward. They had to be, for otherwise others would take their place—there were always others.

Because, if they missed this bus, for whatever human reason of their own—and some did—they would be fifteen minutes late. The next bus would be the Bus of Charon.

For some, that made a difference of life and death. Tardy Status would result in decreased credit, and hence an upset in the regular credit balance, which in turn became a discrepancy in their living resources balance. . . .

And once thrown out of sync, the loss of balance resulted in a spiraling downward trend of varying degrees. In a matter of months of being unable to make up the amounts past due, and to keep up with the normal bills, these people would end up completely cut off from any public help network.

No credit collection agencies. Instead, things were simple. Failure to pay bills within deadlines resulted in services being simply cut off unforgivingly and permanently. For example, to re-open an account with the Electric Company, you had to demonstrate at least three months' sufficient regular income flow, and various penalty fees would apply. But how to survive in the meantime?

Those who failed to pay wouldn't end up on the streets, however. Housing was practically guaranteed, and there was a six month rent payment grace period.

Generosity. But upon closer examination, expediency. For, without electricity, water, or heat, most would become too weak to make it to Work on time (which further reduced their already ailing credit), then too weak to venture outside for groceries, standard non-Interface medications, and other necessities, and finally too weak to rise out of bed.

Toward the end, they would lie in bed, some for a matter of weeks before they died. Eventually they would be rotting in their own filth, unable even to reach the bathroom, and would basically starve to death, slowly in their homes. Few ever took advantage of the six months grace period, since few lasted beyond two months of such agony. . . .

Ah, balance.

About two hundred feet into the block, Nelson paused only for an instant to glance at his watch, just to get a grip on his bearings, to see if he was making good time. Unfortunately, even here balance was the enemy. Slowing down, the hypnotic rhythm of movement that he had built up was thrown off kilter, and he suddenly had to pause longer than he anticipated, gasping for breath, letting himself fall on his stomach upon the concrete, in complete muscular abandon. Behind him, the Crawler immediately following, ran into him, and struck his left ankle and calf painfully, accompanied with an angry grunt of protest.

Nelson did not bother to reply, but cussed him out in his mind, and continued lying on his stomach, gasping. Yes, that felt good. . . . If only he could remain like this forever, not moving. . . .

But the dulled soreness in his muscles, the arthritic agony in his wrists, elbows, and knees, now that he was not concentrating on the superhuman Crawling movement, reminded him of the true state of his body. It reminded him that he could not afford to let go now.

Not now.

Six-forty-two.

Nelson imagined what it would be like to telecommute. But telecommuting was only for the rich. Why not telecommute, work from home, skilled professionals Plugged In comfortably? Because it cost blood money to be connected to the Interface from home. Because unlike the internet, the Interface was a cyberbiological lifeline, the new substitute for health insurance. And while everyone had internet access from public places, only the working ones could pay to be Plugged In. Without that energy few could sustain a full workday.

Nelson allowed his collapsed lungs to balloon outward, to fill with air. And at the same time he used the in-drawn breath like a catalyst to raise himself back on his knees, adjust the slightly misaligned left knee-pad and both the elbow-pads.

Then he started again to Crawl.

Right elbow and right knee. Left elbow and left knee. Every Crawler had synchronized differently, moving limbs and appendages together or apart, with in-drawn breath or with released breath. Nelson had gotten into the habit of moving his right arms and legs together with each expelled breath. In his mind, he counted time. . . .

Breathe in, breathe out.

Lungs sucking air, while elbows jarred painfully against concrete, despite the thickness of the pads.

Walkers moved rapidly ahead, heels striking the concrete. At one point, another Crawler, obviously in a superhuman hurry, shoved him painfully from behind, accompanied by yells of protest from other Crawlers similarly cut off, and passed him.

Nelson ignored him, and continued counting time, continued to move limbs. A slow growing agony had long since established itself in his innards, and now began to jab at his lungs, knifing him, just as he had reached the middle of the block.

It didn't help that from behind him, voices of other Crawlers announced the arrival of the bus at the last stop only two blocks behind them. Voices always traveled faster than the bus, as eager Crawlers yelled out the sighted bus to those ahead of them in line, urging all to hurry. The bus stopped for exactly seven minutes to unload and load passengers, which meant that it was now six-fifty-three.

All of a sudden, Nelson felt something rip inside of him.

The agony was new, fiery cold, and unbearable, and it threw him off, made him lose the count.

It also made him stumble and fall on his stomach, then instinctively roll back and forth, mouth opened into a silent scream.

Something inside him was not right.

The Crawler next in line behind him, a thick, hairy old man, ran into him with an angry grunt, losing his own inner rhythm, and had to make a detour around his collapsed body.

The Crawler then cried "Wipeout!" and immediately the warning was passed on to the back of the line. Angry desperate old bodies started shoving to detour around the collapsed heap of agony curled into a ball that was now Nelson.

"No! No!" he was groaning, "Not wipeout! I'll be okay, just watch me! I'll be okay—"

But they already ignored him, while the single file line had moved a foot and a half to the right of him, effectively shutting him out of their moving stream.

Nelson lay on the very edge of the sidewalk, having nowhere else to roll off, except for the street below. There was no place to Crawl except in that one lane, since there were potted trees at the edges of the sidewalk in regular intervals, and they would effectively block any progress.

He lay, and he thought of his paycheck, and of what he was going to pay off with it. Seconds ticked. He thought of Sandra.

And then he gathered himself, hauling in an unbelievable breath, and willed himself to soar above the agony, above that ripped *something* inside him. Something else angry, beastly, furious, made him think over and over, *Damn me, I will clock in today, I will clock in On-Time...*

Nelson no longer felt himself, his body, but was soaring as he turned himself back on his stomach, stilled for a moment, then rose up on his knees.

Like an automaton made not of flesh but of something else, he moved to the Crawler line, and gasped to the next person moving, "Please let me in. . . ."

He was ignored. The woman with a pinched face, in gray sweats and maroon jacket continued moving onward, eyes stilled ahead of her, as though he were a leper begging for a touch. The man behind her acted the same. And so did the next three. In fact, the Crawler line had picked up speed, was racing now, to catch the bus that would come roaring by them to the stop just ahead, and wait only seven minutes.

Nelson hesitated only for a moment, and then he lunged suddenly, before a small shrunken old man, and cut in just ahead of him. The man cussed, but Nelson did not care—he was soaring in agony—and he threw himself ahead and back into the rhythm of the Crawl.

Only a third of the block left to go. They could see the end of the playground and the adjacent shopping center, with peripheral vision.

A loud roar of diesel engines came upon them suddenly from behind.

It was the bus.

With moans and grunts, the Crawlers picked up speed yet again, if such was possible to imagine. Nelson felt himself overwhelmingly pushed and shoved, as several started to overtake the rest, and their single-file line broke up at last into a chaotic mob of old bodies in various stages of infirm madness and exertion.

Right elbow and knee forward, left elbow and knee forward, pumping. . . .

With a screech, the bus hit the brakes as it pulled up to the stop, doors whooshing open with the hydraulics, and it was six fifty-nine or probably seven exactly. But Nelson didn't dare stop now to check the watch, because—hell, in that moment of the here and now it didn't matter. . . .

Fifty feet left to the stop.

They were suddenly all passing him. . . .

Little old ladies with blue hair and knocked off hats. Shaking Parkinson-ridden old men, grunting like old dry engines that couldn't. All of them huffing, puffing, and incapable of blowing even a house of cards down. . . .

Twenty feet left to the bus stop.

He could see the crowd from feet level, could see the endless legs of the Walkers and the bodies of the Crawlers, as they milled at the edges, waiting for the small group of passengers to exit from the folding doors, thus making room. . . .

His mind was starting to drift, and his body had now felt remote.

Left elbow, left knee, stab of concrete, agony. . . .

There were no Crawlers left behind him. Even the thin little man before whom he had cut back in line, had now passed him, with a disdainful sideways glance, his shallow breath coming raggedly into hissing lungs, little rheumy eyes of triumph— thought Nelson.

He was alone, five feet behind the last Crawler and losing ground.

The bus had finished admitting the Crawlers, and was now allowing the Walkers to board. Which meant, that even if he got to it, it would be almost impossible to find room in the sardine can. . . .

Ten feet left. . . .

Nelson arrived at the hurriedly emptying bus stop, just as he was getting extremely lightheaded, and little sharp specks of color light started to dance before his eyes, signifying that he was about to lose consciousness.

Everything was now in slow motion. The yellow painted lines on the pavement blurred, the concrete screamed at him in hallucinogen shades of gray washed by the first rays of morning sun.

The last three passengers were boarding.

Nelson made straight for the doors, although the Crawler-Wheeler ramp had been retracted, and only the Walker stairs remained. And so, a maniac, he grabbed the last passenger by the legs, clamping on like a dying crab.

"Please," he moaned, "Let me on! Please! I gotta make On-Time!"

His voice sounded alien, like someone else croaking in his stead.

He looked up, disengaging the ankles of the alarmed Walker, and saw a sea of cold faces, a hundred indifferent or hostile eyes.

And then he saw the serious knowing pair of eyes belonging to the bus driver.

"All right, get on," said old Fred Witworth, a graying black-skinned man of African descent.

Fred has been driving this bus ever since he first started using the line. Fred knew him. And Nelson knew Fred, who was also nearing that age. . . .

Fred understood.

And Nelson took in a deep breath of phenomenal relief, and then he proceeded to pull himself up the stairs on his elbows, while several Walkers took hold of him, and started to lift him up. It wasn't charity on their part, of course—they simply didn't want to be late on his account.

Nelson was pulled in full-body, and deposited in the bus, just as the doors whooshed with hydraulics and closed. He lay breathing harshly, specks dancing before his eyes, surrounded by a sea of legs. Fumbling in his back pocket, he finally brought out a worn plastic Senior bus pass, and raised it up for Fred to see. As if Fred hadn't seen it before. Fred nodded silently, acknowledging him.

Then, the floor of the bus beneath them trembled and roared into life, as gears were engaged and the engine screamed like a dervish.

They were moving.

Nelson passed out.

But soon enough, he came to, called forth from his own abyss by a voice of duty. The next forty-five minutes of the trip were a slow dark nightmare, full of stink of gasoline and exhaust, punctuated by dips in and out of consciousness, constant stops for passengers, doors opening and closing, feet shifting all around him. Several times, not being in the designated Crawler section of the bus, he was nearly trampled.

Finally, they had arrived downtown, at his stop. Seven-forty-five, on the dot.

The doors flew open, and the mob of Walkers immediately pushed forward past him, stepping on him. This was a major last stop, and most of the passengers would be getting out here, in the center of commerce where so many of the office jobs were.

Finally, Nelson found himself near the doors. Thankfully the Crawler-Wheeler ramp had been lowered, so he simply moved forward on stiff dead elbows and knees, that had grown atrophied from the forty-five minute pause of inactivity.

The rest of the Crawlers surged behind him.

Somehow, Nelson found himself carried down the ramp by their momentum, and on the hard dust-stained concrete of the business district. His Work building was only a block away, the tall twelve-story high-rise with a prominent bank logo on the very pinnacle. His office was on the sixth floor.

Getting to it was the last hurdle, and the hardest part.

Nelson took a deep breath that pierced him like a sharp blade with renewed agony, and once again began to Crawl.

First, there was the ledge of flat concrete, and then, after twenty feet, hell began.

Cobblestone. Fifty feet of it.

It was decorative, of course—attractive crude slabs of rose-hued granite, that had been a recent architectural addition to the plaza. But it was agony on the elbows, wrists, and knees. Sharp jagged slabs poking into feeble old flesh. . . .

Right elbow, right knee, left elbow, left knee.

Somehow Nelson made it, in a haze of pain-induced stupor. Cobblestone concrete trim ended at the doors to his building. Here, Nelson glanced at his watch, and saw seven-fifty-one.

Nine minutes to eight. He had nine minutes to Clock In, in order to receive a full Work day's credit, and fourteen to receive Near-On-Time.

As it was, he was willing to settle for Near-On-Time.

In the deep-red carpeted lobby, several Crawlers, and a number of Walkers, were hurrying to the elevators.

Ah, carpet! How wonderful it felt on the knees and elbows, even though it was shallow-pile and worn from the many feet covering it every day.

Energized by such a simple positive thing, Nelson doubled his efforts, and with a spurt of hope, moved solidly to the nearest elevator. This was an older building, without special Crawler access, so there were no floor-level buttons to push.

"Floor six, please . . ." he gasped to those who stood nearby.

Someone pushed the round button labeled six, and Nelson mumbled automatically, "Thank you."

His watch read seven-fifty-four.

Another minute later, the elevator arrived.

Nelson was speaking a mantra silently, over and over, begging any Supreme Being that might hear him for fewer elevator stops.

He Crawled in from the deep burgundy of lobby carpet onto the gray coarse pile of the elevator carpet. Others followed him. Elevator doors shut. The floor dipped, then soared, and they began to move.

The elevator stopped on the third floor. His watch read seven-fifty-six.

Four damn minutes.

It stopped again on the fourth floor. Nelson watched an energetic young man in business clothes walk into the elevator, a long metal twinax cable attachment temporarily disengaged and hanging from the back of him, directly from his Cortex Interface. Obviously Plugged-In recently, and adequately charged to Walk between floors, he kept his eyes discretely averted from the Crawlers. Nelson and the two other Crawlers in the elevator watched him with unconsciously angry envy.

Thankfully the elevator skipped the fifth floor.

At the sixth, it opened. Before lunging forward, Nelson desperately glanced at his watch.

Seven-fifty-eight.

He had two minutes to cross the fifteen feet of the corridor, make a turn and open the first door on the left—the door to the office which employed him—and then lift himself to a full upright position to reach the Time Clock. It was located right at the entrance, mounted up on the wall, at Walker level.

Nelson fell into a Crawler sprint.

Left elbow, left knee, right elbow, right knee. . . . Each contact with the floor, a bone-jarring impact.

His breath like a rasping engine, sweat pouring from him, Nelson rounded the corner, then pushed the full weight of his body against the heavy glass door to the office suite 205.

The glass door swung, and the youthful receptionist, Angela Swalls—already positioned at the front desk switchboard, Plugged-In and freshly dressed and made-up—greeted him with a light smile and a glance at the Time Clock, then continued to speak with the caller.

The Time Clock was only a few feet away, sitting up there on the wall, like an owl in a tree. Its LCD display read seven-fifty-nine and forty-three seconds. Its small round Interface Connector beckoned.

Nelson growled, and raced like a spider to the wall. Only three long steps for a Walker. Four for a Crawler.

He made it in a record five seconds.

The most difficult final thing he had to do was stand up.

To do it, and to Plug himself In, he had twelve seconds.

Nelson felt his vision clouding and he pressed gloved palms against the wall, and attempted to rise up on his elbows. Two seconds later, he was on his knees, palms against the wall for support, attempting to grunt his way into an upright position.

Right foot lifted, while all his weight now rested on the left knee.

A moment of superhuman effort.

A stumbling limpness of muscle and bone, giving way before him. Nelson once again lay flat on his stomach.

The clock ticked.

The old bitch could get up and help me, he thought. *But no, Angela would only be happy to see me lose the final balance at last, to see me permanently detached from the System.*

She is probably watching me now with a hidden smirk, and seeing it happen right before her eyes, this thing she is waiting for.

But then, lying on the floor there, with only six seconds left before eight am, Nelson thought of Sandra.

And it gave him power, that thought. More than he had ever had before, an emotional surge.

Nelson raised himself on his elbows, methodically placing palms against the wall, then placed his left foot sole down, and started to rise.

He prayed that his left knee wouldn't give out like his right had, only seconds earlier.

His knee held. Methodically expelling his breath, Nelson placed his right foot down, and then rose up to his full height of five feet-eleven inches. He stood, head spinning, his nose inches away from the Time Clock.

Nelson rested his left palm against the wall, while with his right, he reached out, scrambling, and felt for the Interface Connector at the nape of his neck where the microchip was imbedded, the one that he'd kept tucked into his sweatshirt collar.

While ridiculous infinity stretched around him, he found the twinax, and pulled out the connector, and brought it around and in front of him.

Nelson Plugged himself In just as the Time Clock registered seven-fifty-nine and fifty-nine seconds.

He felt a surge of power. A familiar explosion at the base of his skull. And at the same time, the face of the Clock registered his personal ID in a flash of green, just in that last second before the hour.

And in microseconds, he was growing young. After that initial neural agony of restructuring, came an outpouring of pleasure and relief. His very cell structure had acquired an immense boost, and strength was pouring back into him, as it did every day just after Connection.

"A little too close today," said Angela, smiling at him. She had hung up on the last caller and was regarding Nelson with her thick collagen-lipped seductive bitch smile. He knew how fake it was of course, knew that soon after she Disconnected for the night, she would shrivel up into a seventy-nine year old hag with varicose veins, feather-lips, and a nasty attitude.

But for the moment he didn't care.

Nelson stood up, stretching his renewed young body, while he continued to Charge at the Interface. In about five more minutes he would be able to Disconnect, then go calmly to his cubicle, grab his crisp business clothes with him and take his usual morning shower, after which he would be ready for the Gerendstall presentation and the meeting with the MIS department. He'd only have to Recharge every two hours.

He would Work through the rest of the day, business as usual, and earn the full On-Time Status paycheck.

Then, when five o'clock rolls around, he would clean out his cubicle, place all his stuff in a backpack, and Disconnect.

He would Disconnect for the last time.

On his way home, while still Charged, he would run to the supermarket and do as many chores as possible, also for the last time. Chores that Sandra will now, to some extent, be able to do herself.

Angela can have her snide moment after all, starting tomorrow, when he won't show up at Work ever again.

Because this paycheck will go toward the final installment of Sandra's convalescent home reservation. She'd be guaranteed a whole year there, during which she could recuperate, have regular access to the Interface, even regain a portion of her former financial balance.

As for him, well. He was just an old man who wanted to rest.

Aside from that, nothing else really mattered.

FACES AT THE END OF TIME

They used to say once—they being *homo sapiens*—that love will outlast the end of the world.

I disagree—I being the Point of View that was once based in a *homo sapiens* shell. I know it is not love that will be there when All Comes Together, but hate.

It is almost upon us, the moment when All Comes Together. The heat and pressures of the matter soup around me are indescribable in any quantitative terms at my disposal. The concepts themselves are difficult to grasp, because there is now very little beyond this ultimate pressure.

There is no light. Or rather, light energy is undergoing the same pressure as all other matter, and has been transformed so that it no longer registers on any meaningful scale.

The Point of View that is myself has a great deal of difficulty retaining cohesion. My self-repairing Shields are barely keeping up against the force of the surrounding universe. The Shields are fighting a losing battle in counteracting the subatomic decay that is stripping off layer after layer of particles and crushing them into the heat and pressure and uniformity that surrounds me. And if it were not for the occasional once-in-a-million-light-years twinge of awareness of the Other Point of View, the one across the chasm of collapsing matter—the only other stationary point like myself—this Point of View that is Myself would simply give in to the pressures and collapse also.

But as it is, we stand facing off each other, Myself and the Other, after an eternity of hate, like two fixed islands in a universal concentric whirlpool of energy and matter. Two poles of the universal spindle.

We started out as *homo sapiens*, so-called humans, both of us, a trillion light years ago. What had driven us to hate each other were irreconcilable differences inherent in our individual conscious minds and in our cultures. Cultures were the abstract differentiations self-imposed by groups upon their own immediate environments in which that ancient sapient speck of energy existed in its plural form.

But this is all noise without signal, and I no longer understand or remember what it means.

It is but incoherent dream-chatter of the compiled record that is my past. I have been sapient and mortal once, with trivial concerns. And as such, the origins of my hate now surface randomly and amuse me.

But since I am no longer housed in an organic body but in a durable shell of artificial technology—indestructible for all practical purposes except through the collapse of the universe itself, as is happening at last—since I am immortal, I have the unfortunate means to look back upon Myself and examine everything.

Whatever had caused the hate between Myself and the Other, is lost in the eons of collapsing stars and hurtling wave-particles. All that is of consequence is that we maintain this hate, this adaptation, because now it is our only motivation for existence.

Eons ago we tried to communicate. Occasionally I would send out a blast of focused destructive energy toward the Other. Then I would wait as gas giants bloated around me, hoping to receive Scream Feedback. And once in a while I would be on the receiving end of a similar blast, one which my Shields easily deflected, just as I knew the Other deflected my effort.

It did not matter. What mattered was that we continued to inflict this physical hate energy upon each other, battering each other vigorously at random universal intervals. We were merely ascertaining that the other was still there.

Meanwhile, the universe itself shrank around us.

I knew the Other was drawing closer with each million-light-year blink of the metaphorical *homo sapiens* eye. Neither one of us were moving along the spatial dimension, but the matter and energy between us was compressing and folding in, disproportionately to our own constant selves, in a relativity curve. And as it all compressed endlessly, spanning the atomic distances, we seemed to float closer to each other, until at one dark point I could sense the Other's presence directly, not indirectly through Feedback Loops.

And then, one moment very near the end, Myself and Other were positioned with nothing but the tiny infinitely compressed matter-energy universe to keep us apart. If human terms were to apply here, then the universe could be described as a pearl of infinite density between our lips.

That, and the hate.

We squared off in our consciousness, the Other and Myself. We sensed each other fiercely, with a long-forgotten invigorating swell of joy. It was a triumph of existence to perceive the enemy still so constant, so rarified in material composition, so distinctly *there*.

We now defined the outer edges of the universe by the outer edges of our physical structures. An impossible sensation, knowing that there was nothing beyond ourselves. But we did not dwell on it, using all of our will and being to maintain cohesion.

Since the ancient concepts of shape and color no longer applied in a world of such intense density and contorted energy—and neither did tense—then all Myself can-could-would summon forth out of memories of sensual description is that the Other is-could-be-was my opposite.

The Other had been of the opposite gender from myself in terms of our ancient original bipolar species that had evolved to stand upright on two appendages. He had been male, while I, female. Or maybe, the other way around? And with that ancient image and structure I still perceive us sometimes in these final instants, sentient shapes of matter with distinct curvilinear forms.

The moment was and now is.

The man stands across from me in the void. He is a memory construct of darkness and his repulsive face is before mine, so close that I can see the lines in the skin, the pallor of bared teeth, feel the stir of warm imaginary breath from his cruel human mouth against my cheek. The tendrils of his hair twist and softly fade into the fabric of the vacuum behind him—a vacuum the edges of which he defines.

His eyes are unblinking, his ancient animal pupils round and dark with evil. I face him with an inscrutable killing stare of my own, and in my eyes there is evil also, hard, cruel, merciless, destructive. I know, because I am reflected in his pupils.

For a moment, as the universe presses in, the hate becomes noise, not signal.

And then again I understand and remember what hate is, and I regain my will to be.

"You will die at last, enemy," he says in that moment, and I watch the ugly folds of his lips move and then settle into a deadly gloating smile against the cosmic vacuum.

"You too will die at last, enemy," I reply. A shudder of self-awareness fills me, together with an upswell of joy. This last energy-burst invigorates and maintains me.

I stand, my face against his, not feeling the imaginary body of a woman below, just faces—his and mine. Waves of destructive repulsion-energy, the opposite of gravity, flow between us and the universe, keeping us in a separate phase, setting up domain walls and pronounceable irregularities between our clusters of matter, and thus maintaining our individual cohesiveness.

But eventually, because of the effort spent, I am unable to maintain my objective perspective and the sense of time. It becomes difficult to retrieve even this record of my past. The face opposite of Myself begins to disintegrate, for I and none other am keeping it static with my memories.

My Shields collapse.

As matter distorts further between us, I feel the wrenching pull upon the cohesiveness of my being. I am repeatedly and randomly slammed deep into the various points of the past, into my origins, and I can extrapolate that the Other is subjected to similar forces, as his Shields are destroyed.

The sensation is a pulse of signal and noise, death throes of sentience.

Time and the record of our identities vibrate in sub-atomic waves—faster and faster—and Myself is subjected to the history of Myself repeatedly, in different directions and fragments along my personal temporal continuum.

It is a safe assumption that the same thing is happening to the Other.

And since our history includes both of us, then occasionally we fluctuate along our common timeline.

Eventually the temporal-memory pulses exceed the finest quantifiable distinction. And as the dense pearl of the super-compressed universe acts to dissolve us, the only resistance we offer is the distinction of ancient hate, the challenge to watch the enemy perish first.

And thus we struggle to keep going, to be the last.

Time loses all cohesion soon after, and all effort goes into maintaining the separation between Myself and Other.

Hate is now but the simple distinction of identity. And even hate has no meaning when the subatomic particles of our selves are already mingling, when the matter structures are collapsing under the impossible density.

Our imaginary faces come together, squeezed tight, flattened, our lips pressed violently in an absurd parody of a kiss. And now that we have lost our atomic stability, we are mingling, Myself and Other.

In snatched instants I hurl Epithets of Rejection energy at the Other, and the Other replies erratically with floundering volleys. And now there are only the feeble bursts of this Anti-energy that originates in each of us and is instantly dismantled by the pressure-pearl universe. However it is just enough to keep us in existence, while inevitable atomic dissolution continues, and particles of matter constituting Myself and the Other are ripped off and hurled into the universal whirlpool between us, consumed by anti-particles.

We are rapidly decreasing in mass, Myself and the Other.

Our tiny remnants float along the outer edges of the universe-pearl, orbiting it. It, the universe, also decreases into a single point singularity, ever-gaining density. As we struggle to remain on the boundary of the singularity, Myself realizes that with each Anti-energy burst there is less of Myself left.

The choice to struggle becomes an inevitable tradeoff.

The first things to go are memory constructs. They swirl out like wisps of gossamer, like spiral arms of ancient galaxies, self-referential, and are consumed.

At some point, the last human memory is lost. Human life rushes before me in a blink—a curving reel of ancient film, a curiously poignant metaphor—and with it the connection to the Other.

And then, this memory. Why is this one the last? In it I see Myself running through a green field, a girl with pale hair brilliant underneath the spring sun, a scream of laughter bursting out of me, and the wind drying on my wettened lips. Sun is warm upon my organic human skin, which is warm on its own, without the sun, from the inside. And ahead of me I see the faint perfect curvature of the ancient earth's horizon.

And then no more.

In this last memory there is no Other, no enemy, no challenge.

As sentience is gone, all that is left is matter. And immediately, because there is no more memory of hate, Myself falls apart subatomically, and I never know that the same happens to the Other, as the Other also loses the memory constructs.

Particles of us—the last stable bits of matter—blend momentarily in a final antagonistic exchange, before the final collapse into the universe-pearl.

Our differentiation ends.

The End itself comes softly in the blink of the universal eye, like an exhaled breath. And at that point density collapses all matter-energy into One Particle-Wave and Anti-Particle-Wave Pair.

Our two last separate particles have come together, canceling each other out, to make that one, consisting of Myself and Other and all the Others who had gone before us, and to make *nothing*.

All is *nothing*. But Nothing is All. In that, an ultimate surprise of fulfillment.

Perfection.

But only for a cosmic instant.

For what follows is an intense reversal of momentum in the form of an Explosion containing the energy potential the size of the former universe.

In that burning instant when All is starting to hurtle outward, when every bond of every tiny particle-wave of matter-energy is suddenly ripped from the others once more, there is a weird state of universal silence.

It is a gap of wrenching agony and regret, a silent scream.

Because One is ripped into Many. And now we all feel the forming of the new subatomic empty space—and thus time—between us, and with it we share a common memory of loss that is older than any universe. This memory is the only remnant of the former universe, carried over to this new one. How many times was this memory passed on, from how many universes?

We remember that we all hated and it had kept us from coming together. And we realize too late that it is that hate—its anti-energy potential and resistance momentum—that now keeps us from *staying* together for longer than an instant, that forces us now to begin all over again the pendulum of movement apart.

Hate has caught up with us and now we are hurtling once again, riding its outward-bound force, and remembering for all time what we were denied—a state of perfect union.

We will ride thus, with the primeval blueprint of longing and regret deep in our material makeup, while again matter grows heavy and complex and at some point sentient, while subatomic particles bond and form into atoms which in turn form elements and the fireworks of stars, and life is germinated, and just maybe the hate momentum fades and transforms into a different kind of force.

Then it will be another chance for us, the next time All Comes Together. For he will be glorious, and I might look into his face differently at the end of time.

PORT CUSTODIAL BLUES

There's gotta be a billion words for "shit" around the galaxy. I'm sure of that, because there are at least several hundred words for "shit" that I have personally heard spoken around here in the lavatories, restrooms, bathrooms, sitrooms, voiding closets, elimi-chambers, and other places for excreting living waste here in the lower intergalactic spaceport.

I get to clean up after them, making sure the men's rooms and the women's rooms and the uni-rooms and the multi-rooms are clean, and the facilities are fully functional and attractive to the public.

You wouldn't believe the kind of messes they make. Humans are some of the worst offenders, despite the fact that their elimination process is relatively easy. They just have their number one and number two, liquid and solid waste, and they do it relatively easily into porcelain bowls in little private locked stalls or into small discreet urinal basins. Well, compared to that, the glaziri have a three-day ceremony, and no, I am really not kidding you. They have number one and two and three—third is oil, this thick gloppy completely unscented, thank the gods, lipid waste. Since this species is unable to digest fats but requires them for some peculiar internal lubrication, the fats and oils get broken down into basic lipids internally and have to be filtered though a specialized organ—or so they tell me.

Why do I do this, you might ask? A spaceport janitor's job is an ugly thing, and some people even go as far as to say it's a cruel and unusual punishment.

Why? I am a Cleanser, is why. Teal Wade, human male, 36 standard Sapiens years. You might say I come from a religious sect that believes that cleaning up is sacred, that nothing is too base to handle. You might say it, but I won't use those exact same words—I mean we all have our limits, even Cleansers. And still I get the interrogation treatment from my Boss, who doesn't seem to believe me when I say that I do the job in earnest and pay attention to every detail.

"Did you scrub the stalls, Wade?" says Boss.

"Yeah, I scrubbed the stalls."

"Did you drain the oil?"

"Yes, I drained the goddamned oil."

"For someone religious you sure do cuss a lot."

"Hell, in my religion that kind of thing is just fine."

And so it goes.

Oh, and get this—seeing crazy stuff is one thing but you wouldn't believe the kinds of things I overhear. People give away secrets when they eliminate their bodily waste. I guess it makes it easier for them to concentrate or something, if they also grunt and use expletives as they go. It's also amusing that some of them are very private while others do it in the open. The bashkae sit in a circle around ten elimination holes in the floor and hold tentacles as they open their anuu and relieve themselves of the syrupy thick combination waste product. Bashkae have only one kind of waste. And they get rid of it once a day or even less frequently, often waiting in the wasterooms for hours until another bashkae shows up—the more of them the better—and they all go at the same time, chattering as they do.

On the other hand, the loner waasi pilots completely isolate themselves in their one-person elimi-chamber, and Lord only knows what they do in there, and how it is done. All I know is, when it's time to clean their facilities I have to formally petition their embassy, and some serious-faced waasi comes personally to unlock the elimi-chamber. He stands there and watches me as I go inside and collect the hermetically sealed containers of their waste product and refill the room with clean empty containers. When done, I hand the used waste containers to the waasi, and he marks off in his tablet pad that the room has been sanitized. Beyond that I have nothing to do there, and indeed the elimi chamber is always spotlessly sterile even when it has been used. That makes me think the waasi are bizarre in more than one sense, even though they look rather humanoid.

The other day the Boss sends out a Security Alert to Port Custodial, which is pretty much the whole janitorial and facilities staff cadre. We're supposed to be on the lookout for suspicious stuff. Actually, we're told there has been an incident in the spaceport but we're not told much else. Supposedly there was a shooting at one of the shuttle terminals, or maybe a tube transport tampering. Okay, so most of this is rumor, because Boss never gives us the detail, according to his contract—if he did, he would be exercising witness prejudice, and that would put him in a crappy, so to speak, political situation with the authorities. So all we ever get is a general warning: "Look and listen, keep records of all comings and goings, write down anything unusual, and just record and back up all transactions."

It's really easy to become paranoid, given such a directive, and believe me, I do get cranky and touchy, and I keep an extra gun and charger in the utility cart, in addition to my tool-gun-scanner multibelt.

And now, get this—rumor has it, the incident involved the smuggling of an item of InterGalactic value, and then a clandestine disposal of it in one of the elimination facilities.

So I am willing to bet a standard week's pay that this will end up being a Facilities Purge. We're all gonna have to go and scan and analyze a whole lot of alien shit, just because Boss says so.

Good thing I am a Cleanser, or I'd be howling right about now, like the rest of the janitors. Even as a Cleanser, I admit this would be a hell of a tough job.

Well, I get off shift late tonight, after sanitizing the vragaa express bowl in the main terminal and ticket area—the vragaa eliminate on the go by dumping vapor-fine orange liquid into these little cup-like containers that they immediately discard into a suction slot of the express bowl, and they never stop moving. Of course it helps that the vragaa are like giant Earth slugs. They move slowly, their bulky annelid tentacles barely lifting off the ground, as their underbodies sweep along the floor leaving a long moist streak behind them. So although cleaning the express bowls takes minutes, it takes much longer to actually clean the liquid trail sludge off the floor of the spaceport. Vragaa sludge has to be marked with "wet floor" signs every ten meters, and then you have to go back and dust it with absorbent silica powder that dries it out and the residue can be suctioned with an industrial port-vac. All in all a real hassle. But you gotta do it with a smile, since the vragaa are real sensitive folks.

As soon as I am done, I head to lock up the utility cart, plug it into the portnet for recharging and data sync, then punch out and head home along one of the tubewalks. Home's a small cubicle on the third bottom level of the spaceport, right underneath the pathway of a major transport tube artery. Imagine falling asleep to the sound of eight-ton tube shuttles whooshing on your ceiling every five minutes, while the whole cubicle shakes and wall fixtures rattle in their metal slots. Sometimes the terminal cable gets loosened and I lose portnet connection. Tried taping it to the outlet, but the tape doesn't stick very well to the wall exo-polish, so I ended up moving a storage bin to press it in tightly. The only advantage of this place is that the rent's cheap, and I get a nice Inconvenience Bonus from the tube shuttle company every ten days.

So anyway, here I am, walking along the fourth level hall, about to take a detour to Jilla's Grill and some nice Earth-style takeout. It is dark, and most of the hall-lightcones have been knocked out by some rat kids, and there's laser graffiti everywhere along the metal rib-walls, and it smells like concentrated human piss mixed in with gorti elimi-water and a bit of vragaa sludge—yeah, I would know. Somebody in Port Custodial hasn't been doing their job around here, but it's not my section, so it's none of my business. No one's out and about since it's past nineteen hundred hours, only now and then a late-working straggler like myself. I walk kind of fast, since you never know around here. It's not exactly dangerous according to spaceport Security Zoning but neither is it too safe, if you know what I mean.

The hall starts to curve and there's Jilla's Grill lit up in pink and yellow neon, and just beyond it are the elevators to the lower levels. Jilla herself is a human genetic male who's been modified about a decade ago and is now a redhead with huge mammaries and a great talent for barbecue. Through the clear plexiglass I can see a couple of patrons eating inside, and just as I am about to head straight for the door, I hear running footsteps and human male shouts interspersed with high-pitched flute whistling that passes for agitated talk with the gorti.

They come running around the corner from the direction of the elevators, a man dressed in a gray Fleet pilot uniform and a waddling gorti female. The gorti look like big cumbersome ostriches with a multitude of flute tubes coming out of their cranial protrusions, and although they waddle they are damn fast. And the only way you can tell a gorti female is sort of like those antique Earth cartoons, where the females have these extra-long feminine eyelashes that they'd bat at the male cartoon characters. So a gorti female has these extra-long tube eyelash things. Anyway, they come running straight at me, and the gorti's fluting like crazy, but her translator has been shut off, so all I get is gibberish.

"Are you Port Custodial? We need Security!" says the human pilot.

"Yeah, but off duty," I say. I eye him up and down, and he is not that much to look at, shabby Fleet man, with an older model gun in his holster. But he's young and out of breath; has an earnest face, and a fresh laser raze on the side of his cheek and neck. At the same time I notice the gorti female is also scratched, and she is oozing pale yellow stuff from her head-tubes.

"All right, what happened?" I say, reaching for the dispatch talker at my tool belt.

"We're not sure actually," he says, "but somebody shot at us up in Level 2, where the stores are. Busy area, but we didn't see who it was in the crowd. Strange thing is, no one did. A bunch of glaziri, waasi and bashkae, several humans. We were just getting in the elevators for Jilla's Grill when they got us."

"So why didn't you call Security upstairs?"

The gorti begins to flute like crazy.

"Her translator got broken when they shot," says the man. "And we were already close to the elevator, figured it'd be safer if we ran first and called later. I just happened to try to help her, so they got me too. I am Jordan Rormek, by the way, and this is Maaa Waaa Laialaa."

So I call Security, and report the incident. Turns out, someone has already called it in, but with a different story. According to an eyewitness, the gorti female shot someone first in front of an info-chip dealer, and then waddle-ran halfway down the stores strip, holding on to a tri-info-chip cluster that happened to have on it some very confidential info.

"Look, this is just total bullshit," says Jordan Rormek. "She did not fire at anyone, nor did she steal anything. That info-chip is obviously registered under her own name. We nearly got killed, okay? Do you mind telling Security to come down here, please, so that we can get all of this straightened out in person? Meanwhile, we were heading to Jilla's anyway, so let's just all go inside."

"Fine," I say. "Ladies first." And we go inside Jilla's Grill, following the gorti female. Then I call Security again, and tell them to bring a new gorti translator.

Inside the eatery, Jilla's at the back of the counter, and I see the top of her bright orange head, while her back is turned. There's a hiss against the grill and a mouthwatering smell of synth burger and steak.

We all sit down at the larger table to accommodate the rotund gorti, who is by now only making occasional whistle-noises and looks rather dejected.

The menus slide out of the holders and light up invitingly. I scan one briefly while I watch Rormek take out his nutri-pillbox. I take out my own and snap it in the nutri-holder in my place setting. The nutri works best after a synth meal, not before, so that you get your eating pleasure taken care of, the salivary glands and the stomach juices start flowing, and it's all prime inside for the digestion of the real nutri that keeps us alive. The synth just gets flushed out of the system, like the nothing that it really is. But damn, it sure tastes good and makes life, not to mention a janitor's job, easier. And Jilla's Grill does some of the best synth in the spaceport.

I punch in my order and wait. Might as well get what I'd come here for. Synthajitas with cilantro and onion sauce. But looks like it won't be to go.

Pretty soon Security arrives. Well, not all that soon, since by then we're all eating. Rormek ordered a synth burger with the works, and the gorti is having some kind of cream-colored sludge from the gorti menu. And it actually doesn't smell all that bad. My own synthajitas come sizzling in a frypan, brought over by Jilla herself.

As one Security guy takes testimony from the pilot, the second is attaching the replacement gorti translator. I watch Jilla's friendly smile and bulging cleavage as she arranges my dishes. And then moments later the gorti starts talking Standard.

"This is an outrage! I am Maaa Waaa Laialaa, and this decent human man was only trying to help when someone hit me from the back with a laser shot and damaged my translator not to mention cut my facial tubora. I hurt! No, I don't need a hospital, but still! Your eyewitness is a liar, obviously connected with the incident. Where is he or she, to back up this ridiculous claim? Not only did I not steal, but I lost two portions of a tri-chip worth a lot of money, and although this is registered in my own name, in actuality it is company property and belongs to the conglomerate I work for—"

"Slow down, slow down," says Security One, looking anonymous in his full-body suit and helmet—but I'm guessing he's a human male. "Maybe we'd better have you come to the station with us, and you too, pilot. Both of you need some medical attention, too, do you realize?"

Rormek shrugs, and stuffs the last piece of synth burger in his mouth, then pops two nutris and follows up with a drink. "It's just a scratch. But sure," he says. "And it's the least I can do for this poor lady. I am off duty."

"Heh," I say, chewing my synthajitas wrapped in flatbread. "Off duty. That's my line. Well, good luck to both of you, with whatever it is."

Security Two acknowledges me with a nod. This one's probably a waasi, I'm guessing, since he looks very humanoid-slender and is perfectly silent underneath the suit. No need for testimony from me; they know I'll be including the details in the nightly report for Port Custodial. Not that I even have anything to testify.

Maaa Waaa Laialaa finishes her synth sludge, then also opens a nutri-pill box and takes two into her middle tubora. The brownish pills enter her orifice with a smack, so it seems like she is sucking a lollipop there.

Then they all get up, and the gorti waddles out the door followed by Jordan Rormek and the two Security personnel. When they are gone, Jilla comes back to stand at my side. She shakes her head, saying, "Would you believe any of that? I wouldn't. I think there's more to this thing than we know."

"Yeah," I say and finish up the last of the synthajitas. Then I open my nutri pill-box and pop a couple. I wash it all down with synth beer and then I burp. Ah, that was a good meal, damn.

And then I head home.

The next day there's a portnet message from Boss to Port Custodial, and just as I thought, we're up for a Facilities Purge. I get up, put on the multibelt and uniform, and head out directly to my section. As I'm getting the cart, there's Joe Francie, all ready to head out to his section, his own cart full of waasi containers. He's got it easy, assigned to mostly waasi facilities, and for once, even being a Cleanser doesn't help my mood. On my cart I have vragaa sludge silica buckets and mops and antibacterial spray for three alien species, and boy will I be using all of this today.

"How's it going, Teal?" Joe says. "Bad day for everyone, eh?"

He's expecting me to come back with some positive Cleanser spiel but I just sigh and nod.

"Wow," goes Joe. "Must be real bad to get even you down."

"Yeah, well," I say. "I've got things on my mind. Saw some people who got shot last night. No one seriously hurt, but it is still kind of unpleasant. Sad times we live in."

"Ok, tell me all about it during lunch," Joe says, as he gets up in the driving seat of his cart and heads out to do his section.

I nod, then finish loading the rest of my supplies, and get into my own cart. Then I drive to Section DZ-12 that services Space Gates 1-12 including the big commercial intergalactic hoppers and the passenger spaceliners. Good thing I am a Cleanser, because no one else would have this section, the dirtiest, most heavily used area of the spaceport.

First up on my list are the human bathrooms at Gate 1. These are for the most part pretty decent, except for the usual litter of paper towels and tissues and other human garbage, and when some male has bad aim and misses the bowl or urinal or a female gets drops on the seat. However it is mostly synth-based waste, none of it smelling too badly. And as I spray it down with disinfectant and wipe it off and mop the floors all around, I say the Cleanser prayer of gratitude for a relatively easy job. Though now and then I get a stall which has been used by a newly arrived Earther who's had real biological food for dinner, and the waste leaves a malicious smell. That's when I get out the heavy-duty air freshener. In the meantime, since this is a Facilities Purge, I check every millimeter of the place carefully as I clean, and finally program the plumbing to redirect all waste to the central Custodial processing and analysis facility.

All in all, I am done pretty fast, and next up is Gate 2, with the bashkae wasteroom. This one is usually not too bad either. I knock politely, but unlike the human bathrooms I go in right away, since there is always a party—at least a bashkae or two or three gathered, waiting for a crowd so that they can all eliminate in a group. Sure enough, there are three of them inside. They crouch over the elimi-holes, tentacles joined tightly with their neighbors', and smile at me with their three-lipped mouths, then continue their lively conversation with each other; someone told me once that they discuss philosophy while they wait. I end up working around them, but it doesn't bother them, and it's fine with me. When done washing down the floor around the elimi-holes and their lower appendages, I program their waste redirection into the main facility.

Lunchtime comes soon enough, and I am nearly halfway done with my section, having gone up to Gate 5 and cleaned three more alien facilities and the long hallway and all the trash receptacles along the way. I meet up with Joe for a quick bite at one of the spaceport snack bars and we talk about it all.

"I really want to know what's going on," Joe says. "Supposedly it's a missing tri-info-chip. Just like the one you told me about from your incident. But get this—it's not just corporate info, but they say there's a Fleet-level military secret or two stashed away in one of them three chip modules."

"Interesting," I say, chewing my sandwich.

Joe slurps his Cosmos-Cola.

"Yeah," goes Joe. "That'd be something if you or me found this thing. Wonder if there's a reward."

"Sure there's a reward," I say. "There always is. It's like the lottery, someone's gotta win big."

Joe slurps the ice dregs of his drink and laughs. "You know, Teal, for a moment I begin to understand you Cleanser people. This kind of motivation at least makes sense. So let's go, man! Lunch's over, time to hit the garbage and look for jewels!"

With that he gets up, dialing his dispatch to say he's clocked back in, and off he goes.

I wave him off with a nod, and calmly finish my sandwich. Synthbacon on rye with lettuce and tomato hits the spot. And Joe, poor bastard's got it all wrong. Being a Cleanser I am not in a hurry to profit, so I take my usual time, then get back on the job. For the rest of the afternoon I work with calm precision and perfect attention to detail. Purification for its own sake is where I'm at.

Throughout the shift I call dispatch for news, to see how the Facilities Purge is progressing. Looks like so far they went through several tons of waste, but didn't find what they were looking for.

"Still nothing," says Mardio, today's dispatch. "But I want you to take extreme care with the glaziri facilities at Gate 8. Be sure to check every nook and cranny."

"I always do," I say.

"Well, today you're gonna check it twice," says Mardio. "Boss's orders. Looks like they might have a lead."

"The glaziri are on their third day of the Ceremony today," I mention. "It might be busy there."

"Exactly. That's when they actually go. And as soon as they do, you localize the waste in the plumbing perimeter and radio-mark it before the redirection."

"Say what? You want me to put a radiation trace on their shit?"

Mardio is laughing. "Yeah. And also their liquid and lipid waste. Radio-mark all three."

"Holy crap!" I say.

"You can say that again, Cleanser!"

And that's exactly what I end up doing. I go in the glaziri exo-chamber, past lean bird-like vaguely humanoid shapes dressed in primary colors, and I gently obtain permission to lift up and examine all their exo-bowls. The exo-bowls are lined up in three neat rows, with the nearly colorless liquid waste on the left, the rich amber oil in the middle, and the multi-colored solid on the right. Votive lightcones are burning at each end, and a female glaziri, with a slender but kind of sensual body wrapped in green silk-like fabric, stands at the end of the chamber, reciting the Liberation and Elimination Anthem.

I get a bit distracted by her but never miss the contents of a single bowl. Ignoring me, the glaziri stand at the outer perimeter, each having filled all three bowls from a central organ inside their general stomach area. Their waste smells pleasantly like deeply soggy Earth wood, slightly musky. Without disturbing the ceremony I discreetly point a safety-capped micro-radiation tool at each bowl. When the glaziri empty their bowls into the three plumbing units later, it will all be marked and will be easily identifiable at Port Custodial's analysis facility.

I find nothing, of course, and leave the more high-level analysis up to Custodial.

Pretty soon I am all done with my section, which means I would normally be done for the day, but not on a Facilities Purge day. We all have to report with our carts and our equipment, and get scanned and analyzed, in case we are ourselves contaminated in some way. This is standard procedure, but I always find it a bit insulting, seeing how I am so impeccable in my work.

I drive the cart over to Port Custodial Headquarters all the way on Level 1, along curving tunnel corridors, honking politely at pedestrians and flashing the caution lights. When I get there, I see a dozen other carts, and more arriving. Joe waves to me and we all head into the dark warehouse area for self-scanning. Afterwards we'll get to see Boss.

"Found anything?" says Joe, as we roll along slowly, double file.

"Nope," I say. "You?"

"Nothing."

"Damn."

Then it's my turn to be scanned, and I pull the cart onto the conveyor belt and we cruise past the industrial strength sensors at three meters a minute.

I am in the middle of a very deep relaxed yawn when the Red Alarm goes off as a viral sensor passes through me.

Goddamn it to hell. My mouth falls open in shock and then all kinds of other alarms and lights go on and off, and Security comes running and surrounds me. They point micro-scanners at me and immediately locate the object in my abdominal area. Actually it is now in my lower intestine, and will probably be passed the next time I use the bathroom.

"What the hell," I keep mumbling, as they firmly escort me to an analysis chamber, and here I get questioned while a bright light shines at me and a lie detector is attached to my pulse points.

After several questions it is apparent that I am telling the truth.

"Mr. Wade," Boss himself questions me, "you appear to have swallowed one of the missing tri-info-chip modules from the Ellron-Galactic Corporation which is currently involved in a

political-military scandal that is about to hit the news on a
Galactic scale. We presume innocence, but what is your
explanation, please?"

I sit in the chair, unrestrained, except for the intensity of
stares upon me, and the Security staff all around me, armed and
trigger-ready. Jeez, talk about pressure.

"I don't know," I say weakly. I am dry-mouthed. "Shit, I
really just don't know."

"How about this," says Boss. "Did you swallow any nutri-
pills recently?"

I frown and scratch my forehead. "Why, sure, as usual, at
every meal. Ate breakfast and lunch today. You can ask Joe
Francie there, we had lunch together. . . ."

A medic steps forward and says quietly, "Not today. The
location of the chip inside your intestines indicates that the time
of consumption was most likely to have been some time
yesterday."

Jilla's Grill. The thought strikes me, and so I tell them how
I ended up having dinner with the pilot and the gorti female.

"I can't believe it!" I say. "They must've switched my nutri
pill-box! That female gorti seemed a bit suspicious to me, and
the human also, and she claims to have lost her tri-info-chip.
Does she work for Ellron-Galactic?"

Boss looks at me, then says. "Actually she does not. The
gorti female mugging incident is unrelated to this, except for the
coincidence of missing tri-info-chips in both cases. And neither
does the pilot. He is an honest Fleet man, and both were
thoroughly identity-checked yesterday, and came out spanking
clean."

"So then," I say, "who can it be—"

And then it comes to me, at the same time as Boss says,
"It's Jilla Orsweq. Did you know that Jilla's Grill got startup
funding many years ago from Ellron-Galactic?"

"Well I'll be damned!" I say. "She was serving me
synthajitas at the table. . . . I'll be damned!"

The medic grins. "Not a problem, Mr. Wade. Take this laxative, and believe me, minutes later no dam can stand against it. The bathroom is right around the corner."

And so I pass the tri-info-chip and get to watch my own crap getting carefully processed in the lab next door. They find the fake nutri-pill and, sure enough, inside is a tiny tri-info-chip module. Later that day, the second piece is discovered somewhere else on the spaceport, stashed away in a bag in one of the trash bins. But the third piece is nowhere to be found. The irradiated glaziri post-ceremonial waste is processed to no avail, and Jilla Orsweq is taken into custody, then released on bail since the proceedings can't go on until the three module pieces are connected and the full infoset can be read.

Jilla's Grill gets shut down temporarily, then re-opens for business, about which I am ashamed to admit, I am glad. Always did like Jilla, even though she pulled that number on me, thinking to hide the chip with someone like myself, who's above suspicion, since a janitor's own waste would be the last place anyone'd look. While the authorities continue searching, Port Custodial is asked to do at least three more Facilities Purges over the next ninety days. Still nothing.

Eventually, almost a Standard six-month later, they locate the chip on a shuttle heading, of all places, to the bashkae system, at which point it's out of our jurisdiction. And then it all makes sense.

The authorities had the right idea, but the wrong species. It pays to know about your galactic neighbors, even their bathroom habits. If only we'd known this all along, we'd never bothered with the glaziri and their extended ceremony.

Turns out when bashkae sit around their elimination holes and hold tentacles, it's not just for moral support. They are able to pass waste from one bashkae to another, in a naturally occurring bodily function. The bashkae home world is very arid and nearly barren, and the bashkae have evolved to conserve resources to the point of recycling their own waste in the bodies of others, to supply necessary nutrients. So that when the bashkae sit around in our spaceport wasterooms, they are capable of passing around objects indefinitely to one another, and we would never have found anything without actually scanning them one at a time, not just their waste. As a group— well, let's just say that bashkae play one hell of a game of Hot Potato. And they make great smugglers.

Well, you live and learn.

Damn, but I love this job.

THE ICE

Something will happen as we go down to the planet.

Even now, Wisahkh is below us, orange, glorious. And yet, I must remain silent.

Not because I am cruel or perverse, or because I do not feel the same way as you. But because I am a Voice out of Time. I lurk in the true silence which fills the gaps *between* moments of our life—the homogeneous dream fabric that holds them all together and allows me to hold all moments at once.

Thus, even if I try to verbalize it, to explain, you will not hear me.

To hear me, you must stop your life *now*. Allow the ephemeral clamor of the world to slide past you, and listen with your focused attention, not your auditory senses.

Focus on one and ignore all others. Time, being a unit of measure, marks the evolution of imagination into memory. It is nothing.

Therefore, stop counting. Cease measuring even the spaces between your breaths, step aside time, and you have the moment.

And in that moment you have me.

The surface of Titan was golden ice. After the opaque space view from orbit, after cutting through the nearly impenetrable cloud layers, it suddenly reflected back the sol and

Saturn—not hard and mirror-bright, but through thick luminous fog. It was like looking out from the heart of a glowing paper lantern, or a frosted tree ornament of orange glass. Who would've thought?

Captain Conrad Ehl stared blankly at the digitized view of the orange-gold planet on the small video display of the e-system that was lodged in the back of the seat before him.

He did not want to be here. Not on this ice hell of frozen methane, ethane, and water.

He glanced occasionally at the obese form of the Oracle that occupied the front bench-seat, taking up the space of two people.

The woman was a shapeless mass, covered by dark robes of some kind of natural plant-spun material. Her face was a white moon floating in the darkness of her form, covered by the wimple of her so-called order.

Her eyes appeared closed.

Ehl's second officer Favi Markos was muttering under his breath, checking the readings. "Sir, in four more minutes we will be in ideal position to land at the Warren Base."

"Noted," said Ehl. And then he cleared his throat loudly, and addressed the shapeless woman-form. "Oracle, we are about to start the landing procedure."

The woman opened her eyes. They were like that planet below them, pale brilliant golden ice. They focused on Ehl, and annoyingly he noted how even now she never looked directly at him, but beyond him, through the back of his scalp and out, somewhere timeless.

"Good," she said. "Very good, Captain Ehl, thank you."

Her lips moved like thin flaps of some alien organic mass, and her voice was without tone.

Ehl looked away, repulsed once again, but maintaining protocol. There was no way he was going to cause an interplanetary legal incident by in any way offending this so-called Oracle, someone of the highest deistic position in the Colonialis. Even if she was an offensive slab of—

He induced his thought to terminate. It was rumored, an Oracle had the ability to read thoughts. Which was superstitious nonsense, of course, but he was not going to take any chances, even if these people were not religious fanatics.

He had his orders.

We are about to float down. At first, we will begin to land softly like bubbles of iridescent benzene upon the frozen surface of Wisahkh. It looks unblemished, perfect now, no details from this distance.

As always, I'll suck in my breath. For, at the very first instant before landing, gravity will be manipulated, and the bottom will fall out from underneath us, and we will swoon . . .

And then, we float down gently the rest of the way.

Weightless.

And then. . . .

The braking subsystem engaged, and Ehl felt space vertigo, as it always happens in those initial seconds of landing.

"One hundred seventy-three kilometer erratic equatorial winds, sir," reported Markos suddenly. "I recommend we make another orbital circumference pass, this is not a good time to come down."

"How so? The weather system reported a fair reading only within the last hour."

Markos made an apologetic face. "Sir, like I said, very erratic. Atmospheric pressure is normally 50-60 percent that of Earth, 1.5 to 1.6 bars. It is mostly nitrogen and hydrocarbon elements, but a wild soup. Remember the screens upon screens of map sequences I showed you on the Main? Those sequences of the landing site were taken in a single 15.9-earth-day period that constitutes a Titan day."

"I thought the region that had been mapped was a planetwide range!" roared Ehl suddenly, feeling the one moment of his life when a fatal mistake is suddenly acknowledged by the self, and responsibility slams down, inevitably. "Are you telling me that was all a map of one coordinate?"

And then, not waiting for Markos' response, Ehl cried, "Abort landing!"

Stupid idiotic mistake. A tiny slip of his attention. Ehl hated himself in that moment, himself, that woman in the front seat, this damn planet.

"Yes, sir!"

Markos signaled an interrupt, then called the secondary control station in the engine room, where Zibaida Lorensen was perched like a slim praying mantis from native earth, over the Thrust and Brake.

Lorensen responded flawlessly. She logged the interrupt not a second later, and yet, that was too late.

Something began to shudder all around them. The ship's hull felt strange, for lack of better words. Gravity surged chaotically in an elliptical field around them, as the Brake engaged.

In the front, the giant woman who occupied two benches slowly and inevitably closed her eyes again.

It is happening now. Flashes of fire, as it will happen, and flashes of calm ice behind. Discrete drops of moments splattering down in a torrential rain of events, forming a new causality . . .

I see the moment of explosion approaching. It is coming closer . . . It is almost here.

It is here now.

The hull was rocked by a silent explosion of the outer vacuum perimeter core of the tail end. As the ship fell apart at the seams, two small internal kernels of it collapsed into distinct self-contained ecosystem units, joined with a flexible safety tunnel cable. Together with the debris, they plummeted down like two beads on a string, through the atmosphere of gale-force nitrogen winds.

But it had not been the winds at fault. The ship's own system malfunction caused an internal fault, at the moment of Brake interrupt.

Ehl gripped the handrests of his chair with a bloodless hold, while multiple gravity patterns came in waves, and he felt bile rising. Instinctively he wanted to freeze and ride it out, but he knew he had to take care of the passenger. And so he stumbled forward, where the woman-lump had frozen to her place on the seats, and for the first time he took a hold of the mass that was her body, feeling something soft and boundless give under his fingers, and then ignoring that, he applied the safety harness release that came to envelop her in a cocoon of plastic buoyant layers, up to her neck.

"We are falling, forgive me, Oracle," he muttered uselessly. "For your own safety, I do this, you must understand. . . ."

And when she turned her eyes at him, they were calm, wise, and very sad.

"Be it as it must," she replied. Her wimple hood fell back, revealing pale hair gathered tightly over a round skull.

He watched it, as the illusory feeling of ground generated by the artificial gravity, fell from under him completely, and the long descent to ice hell came to a sudden terrible impact-end.

I am awake. I am lying on my side, for apparently the ship came down without a frame of vertical-horizontal reference. The cabin is nearly dark, except for the emergency lights, one on the ceiling—which used to be the bottom middle of the left hull wall—and another light is right behind my seat where I cannot see it, and which is now on the ground.

It is quiet. But I know they all live, because the captain is shifting at my side. Yes, he is still holding me bodily, despite his aversion, while his other officer is sprawled somewhere silently, in the front. . . .

Luckily for us, there had been no breach—as I knew there would not be. We are self-contained and safe for the moment, safe against the winter of the surface, outside.

Ehl felt intense but bearable pain in his upper left arm, from the impact of the fall against some section of the panels near his seat. There was only faint emergency lighting, and he felt the massive woman at his side, breathing.

"You okay?" he asked, starting to rise, keeping his face impassive from the pain, never giving any of it away.

"I am fine," she said, moving up and beginning to unravel herself out of the safety harness material.

"Markos! Report!" said Ehl, his voice automatic, not so much expecting a technical answer, but to get a living response. Then he saw the form of his prime officer lying motionless.

Ehl walked the few steps, wincing internally at the pain in his own shoulder, and then kneeled to check the fallen man for damage.

Markos's chest rose and fell. He seemed intact. At Ehl's touch, his eyes came open slowly, then focused. Groaning he tried to sit up.

"Sir . . . the Thrust and Brake section—Lorensen is still there, trapped, together with Niva and Frayne. We need to check, we need to—"

"I know. Stay still for a moment." Such a calm voice. Ehl surprised himself.

He then made his way in the grey twilight to a series of controls, and tried to access the e-system.

Finally, he had something—the bulk of the e-system was down, but the backup mailer responded. And so he signaled the Thrust and Brake section, signaled Lieutenant Zibaida Lorensen, Second Lieutenant John Niva, Third Lieutenant Steven Frayne.

Minutes of silence went by.

The Oracle wordlessly lifted her bulk and then made her way to assist Markos to a full sitting position on the floor.

The captain is at a great loss. I can almost read his thoughts, his sense of impossible failure. I want to tell him not to worry, that in about five more minutes Lorensen will respond via the e-system, but I cannot do that. I am saving up my plausibility for the other thing. That which will happen in about an hour. I need to prepare well my explanation.

The e-system signaled a message at last, and Ehl heard the ringing voice of Ziba Lorensen.

"I am sorry, Captain, the malfunction was unforseen, and it had nothing to do with the Brake interrupt itself. One of the sub-systems had a time-out which resulted in a failure cascade. I am extremely sorry. We'd checked and double-checked—"

"How are you, Lieutenant?" said Ehl, breaking through her protocol response. "Anyone hurt?"

"All intact, sir. Frayne fell down and scratched himself, and Niva's spotless. We're simply trap-sealed here." There was forced laughter.

A minor temporary weight of relief came to flood him.

"Excuse me, captain?"

He turned to see the Oracle standing behind him. She was taller than he imagined. Her voice was gentle, and she put her hand on his shoulder, the one that was sprained, the one that he was pretending did not exist.

"Your shoulder. Let me help you with that," she said.

How did she know?

Ehl stared at her, then decided this was no time for heroics.

"Thank you," he said. "But in a moment. First, we need to verify our bearings, see how much damage the ship has taken, see where we are, and how much hope we have."

She nodded, and stepped away, allowing him to proceed.

Despite his injury, the captain is very efficient. He and his dazed officer have determined the extent of the damage, and have determined that the cable-tunnel connecting the two ecosystem modules is safe to open, to merge the crew.

They have also determined we are not too far from Warren Base, having fallen safely on the outer equatorial plain.

Soon, I will have to tell him.

After the proper safety checks, the tunnel-seal opened, and Zibaida Lorensen attempted to crawl the tunnel from ecosystem module B to the main module A. She made it, after 30 minutes, moving a centimeter at a time, checking the circumference of the tunnel for weaknesses, and had to stop at one point, where the tolerance showed a weak spot, and the temperature reading was in the -40 Celsius and falling, headed quickly toward the -178 Celsius surface temperature mean.

The insulation here must have been breached, but for now it would hold, so she noted the spot, and applied thick layers of sealants, before proceeding forward.

Finally Ehl heard a remote knocking on the cabin door, and he released the seal, and here she was, Lorensen herself, grinning with her white teeth and pulling her hood back to reveal wiry dark hair.

"Good to see you, Lieutenant," said Ehl.

"Likewise, sir," she grunted, then came into the cabin, pulling behind her a small but heavy load of salvaged equipment.

"What's the situation of the Thrust and Brake? Our control interlock is down, so I cannot see it online."

"It's all out, sir, sorry to say," she replied. "The two guys are messing with it right now, but I am pretty sure it's dead as a rock."

"Captain?"

Ehl and Lorensen both turned to see the Oracle hovering behind them.

"Captain, please, you need to tell the remaining two crew members in the other module to immediately come here."

"Why?" said Ehl.

"There is going to be a problem. In exactly 15 minutes, there will be another explosion, this one internal. The explosion will damage module B. You need to consolidate the crew, move all the remaining supplies here, including the extra oxygen stores."

"How do you know this?"

She stared with intensity. "No time now, please. Do as I say, captain, trust me on this. Please. No time!"

"What the hell . . ." muttered Ehl, but then, moved quickly to access the e-system backup mailer, and sent a priority urgent message.

"Emergency! You have less than 15 minutes to abandon module!"

There was no need to go into detail, they would know how to react.

Sometimes I am precise to the millisecond. Sometimes not. This is one of the times where I doubt whether I had seen the moments raining, whether it is to be now or days later.

But there can be no chances taken, if this is to work.

Niva and Frayne came crawling through the tunnel within nine minutes, carrying behind them the rest of the supplies. The door was once again sealed, and then, like clockwork, 6 minutes later came the explosion. They all knew it because the e-system backup mailer severed the connection with module B entirely, and the external sensors showed the temperature outside the sealed door in the tunnel plummet suddenly.

They were now completely encapsulated in module A.

Frayne who had medical expertise, went to work on Markos, who had suffered a serious concussion, and then deftly set the captain's dislocated shoulder—while Ehl bore it stoically.

Next, Lorensen and Niva assisted the captain in setting up radio equipment. They had a one-way emergency transmitter that would contact the Warren Base, and help should arrive soon.

Ehl and the crew members threw occasional odd glances at the corpulent woman, who once again sat motionless in the corner of the cabin, and out of their way.

Eventually, Ehl stepped away and approached her. "Thank you for warning us," he said. "I owe you an apology for being skeptical about your status, Oracle. One thing I want to understand however—if you can predict the future, if you knew this was coming, why in all hell didn't you warn us about the landing?"

The Oracle signed. "This is indeed a fair question," she said. "Everyone always asks us why we are selective in our revelations. Why we play god with the fates of all, why we presume to make life and death judgments and decisions."

"Yes," he said quietly. "Why do you? What kind of a crapshoot game is this for you?"

"Not a game," she relied, "but a disease. You cannot imagine what it is I see every moment. I see all possible futures raining down, all possible choices and repercussions. I am faced with making decisions that in turn create other decisions and other terrifying complications, so that for all practical purposes I am living each moment in agony. And all is beyond my control. . . ."

"It still does not explain why you did not even try to help us with the landing."

"I know," she replied. "I could not. That is all I can say. I had no . . . strength."

Ehl stared at her, frustrated anger beginning to fill him, a sudden violent outburst ready to flare.

But he controlled himself, and merely said, "Tell me then, will we survive this ordeal?"

"Yes."

Her answer was not hesitant, did not involve any pause.

But a sudden sick moment of doubt entered Ehl. What if she was lying? What if she merely said this to placate him, withholding the true information to save her own self?

"Should I believe you, Oracle," he said icily, "Should I trust you now?"

"I cannot tell you what you must believe," she replied. "When it comes down to it, belief and skepticism are always up to you."

And then Lieutenant Niva came near them, wiping sweat from his forehead, and he said, "Oracle, if you don't mind, I would rather not know. If I am to die, it will not help me to know how it happens."

I want to tell him, that crewman, that it is a wise choice not to know. He is lucky to have that choice. But I can see captain Ehl watching us both with barely held fury. And I am suddenly afraid to tell him that one last thing. Especially now.

And yet, I must.

The emergency transmitters were successfully deployed, and all they had to do was wait for help to arrive from Warren, maybe even within 50-100 hours. They had plenty of supplies to last them for at least 2 Titan days, or a little over an earth month, and if carefully rationed, for twice that amount. Oxygen was also plentiful, and if that failed, they could somehow tap the ice-atmosphere from the outside which contained traces of rarified oxygen mixed in with a nitrogen-methane cocktail of other gases to keep them breathing slowly through filter-masks that would harvest the oxygen and strip the toxic elements.

"Oracle," said Lieutenant Frayne approaching her. "Here are the rations. Please forgive our lack of a better menu. No appetizers tonight."

He grinned casually, unlike the rest of the crew, and handed her a sealed packet, and a plastic eating utensil. In the semi-twilight of the emergency light, he then sat down cross-legged on the cabin floor, and opened his own portion, then hungrily began to spoon the contents into his mouth, wiping a dark mustache.

"I know your kind," he said after several moments. "My sister is an Oracle too. I know how that is. It makes you nuts. She is now on Colonialis, somewhere out there, hiding from the whole world, just like you are. Except that you chose to come down to this lonely ice place, while she chose the anonymity of the Colonialis crowds, to escape from the . . . infinite possibilities."

The Oracle nodded slowly at him, and then opened her ration packet, and silently began to eat.

This time I must consume as much as possible of the high-calorie food. It makes me gag now, and yet, I know I must, for this is the last set of moments before the inevitable. I fill myself with carbon compounds, protein and carbohydrates, like they all do, only this once, for strength.

Ehl watched the woman eat austerely, and he could almost sense a rhythm to her spare movements, to the swallowing gulps in her throat. . . .

She finished the single ration packet, then remained motionless.

It was at that moment that Lorensen stepped away from where she stood, leaning against the one sealed door of their cabin, and put down her half-finished ration pack.

She then ran down her hands against the surface of the door, and said a curse.

"Shit," she said, gasping. "Captain, quickly, check this out, here, temperature variance!"

Ehl looked up from his task.

"Here, sir!" continued Lorensen, "Here, just at the seal lines, I feel seeping cold! It's supposed to be the same all around the seal lip-lines, but look, here it's noticeably colder!"

Niva and Frayne stopped eating. While everyone stared, Ehl rose from his seat, and quickly put his hand on the spot which Lorensen indicated.

"Shit . . ." he said, after an intense silent moment, "Hot damn shit! We've got a leak!"

"You mean, cold shit," said Frayne, then put his food down also. "Well now, look what you've done, sir, captain, thanks for ruining my dinner."

And then Frayne put his hands on his forehead and sleeked his dark hair back. "We've got a leak," he echoed. "There goes . . . there goes our fucking life."

I am about to tell them. First, I must allow their natural panic to work itself out, followed by anger and by denial. And then, when they've sunk to the utmost level of despair—but not a second earlier, or they will still remain defiant—I will speak the truth at last.

The whole thing.

Ehl and Frayne measured temperature variance at the leak area for at least an hour, to verify the escape rate. They noted that despite the application of many layers of sealants, the area of cold increased, and the degree of cold climbed steadily. When their calculations were complete, Ehl announced impassively that there were about 12 hours left until the heat loss in ecosystem module A reached critical levels.

Which meant, having lost the thermal protection, in 12 hours they will be subjected to the impossible temperatures of the outside surface of Titan.

Temperatures significantly below the threshold of human life.

Thermal spacesuits were handed out, but they would not be enough, knew Ehl with a grim pang, for even with the added layer of insulation, the heat will eventually escape, buying them maybe another hour of slow freezing agony.

They will either be rescued within the 12 hours, or they will die.

The moment is at hand. Oh how I had dreaded it, for the first 2 sol years, how many misgivings were there, and trepidations. It is very similar to preparing for one's own execution, counting down the moments, seeing sprinklings of possibilities branch out and this one being the one certainty, the one that could not be avoided.

But now, the moment is here, and somehow I am no longer afraid at all.

"Help will come!" Lorensen was saying, as she stomped around the cabin shivering lightly, to work up her circulation. "You'll see, they will be here, knocking on the seal door in an hour or two. I swear to all goddamn gods—"

"Quiet, don't call gods names. They may be the only chance we've got," said Niva. Only, it was apparent he had resigned himself to it, and sat in a locked position on the floor, his knees raised high to his chin, his hands gripping the ankles.

Ehl was making himself busy with the transmitter, re-broadcasting the message on different frequencies, in a kind of stubborn futility that can sometimes reassure.

"Rescue will come," said the Oracle calmly.

"Of course they will," said Frayne, lying prone on his back on the floor, with hands tucked under his head in the pose of a casual dreamer. "They will come to find us fucking popsicles, good enough to suck on."

"Shut up," said Lorensen.

In the meantime, the Oracle got up from where she sat, for the first time.

And then she began to strip.

"What the hell are you doing? You suicidal?" muttered Niva, as he stared at her with incredulity.

My insulated outer robe comes off, and I feel the already chill air of the cabin strike my thin shift, and goosebumps breaking out. Air comes stifling in my lungs, more from the anticipation of intensity than of actual cold. I stand looking at their confused shocked faces. Each one of them is frozen already, stilled in their own moment. All I have to do is convince them to still even farther, to step out of time and join me.

It is the only way they will survive.

Ehl watched the impossible thing before him. This Oracle, this woman had lost her mind.

"What are you doing?" he whispered, abandoning the transmitter, coming to her side. "Put that back on right now! You can't give up—"

"No," she said. "It is true, none of us can give up. And what we will do is survive. But—there is only one way we can do it, and I will teach you how."

"What do you mean?" said Lorensen, stopping her shivering.

Frayne lifted his head, and stared, a sudden focus coming back to his eyes.

And then the Oracle surprised them all, and turned and pointed at Markos, suffering from a concussion, who was half-lying, propped up by some packs against the cabin wall.

The emergency light made eerie shadows of contrast against his vacant face, half-conscious no matter how they tried keeping him awake, so as not to slip into a coma.

"He is your example," said the Oracle. "He is easy. See how abstracted he is?"

"Yeah, he's neither here nor there, barely breathing," said Niva.

"Rather, he is living the moment." The Oracle smiled then, for the first time. "He is unable to hold on to a track of thought, to any continuity, and that is what saves him now. He lives in the immediate present. And he can thus *hide* from his body, from its needs, hide in the spaces that are beyond the fabric of measured time."

"What the hell are you talking about?" said Ehl.

But Frayne got up suddenly, saying, "I know. . . ."

And he began stripping also.

"Sir," Frayne was saying, as he pulled off his upper shirt, then his pants. "She is trying to get us to form a single unit of body heat, and then, after we come into close contact, we will use our combined clothing and all the blankets and wrapping material available, to wrap around ourselves in multiple lifesaving layers, including our heads, making a common cocoon."

"Okay," said Lorensen. "That makes sense. But there will still be thermal escape in any non-fully sealed area. This will merely prolong our survival, not guarantee it."

"No," said the Oracle, "There will be no thermal weak areas, and air will not escape."

She paused, and as the understanding finally came to Ehl, she finished. "Because you will not be breathing. You too will only live in the moment."

It is not perfectly true, what I tell them. They will be breathing, yes, and I also. But it will be so slow, so minimal, that for all practical purposes we will appear comatose, our lifesigns down to a minimum. And as a result, body temperatures will drop also. We will stay that way a long time, far longer than would otherwise be possible.

And in the meantime, they do not know it, but my body will keep a higher temperature.

The Oracle's lukewarm boundless body presses against mine. Even now, it is cooling. Somehow, throughout this procedure, my original revulsion had transformed impossibly. I am now shocked to find her glorious, and as great in all senses of the word as this planet. Except, she is ice that soothes, that keeps life by slowing down all processes.

Ice buys time.

The others are also here; at all sides, I can feel them. We are a mass of humanity, a single entity of many limbs, yet no limbs at all.

I feel the slow breathing deep in her chest, and somehow I align my own breathing with hers. We all do.

She is the Timepiece. We must synchronize, she had taught us. And then, we must forget time altogether.

At first, I recede softly. . . . But then, just as suddenly, I panic. I am afraid. My heart bucks against my ribcage in rebellion, as the fear brings me out of the moment into terrible continuity.

But then I allow peace to resurge in place of fear. Continuity which is time, fractures once again, dissipates. I focus upon her boundless unreal warmth—which is in fact cold, and growing even colder—and her heart, which is slowing. And in focusing I lose all else.

I lie against her, and hear the hearts of others. We are all one Timepiece now. I forget who I am, forget the meaning of Conrad Ehl, and simply breathe, softer, slower. . . .

One 384-hour day hence, the rescue team from Titan's Warren Base located the remnants of the crash-landed Colonialis vessel from the Main. Among the debris buried by a new layer of methane and water snow, only one ecosystem was left partially functional, but the temperature inside was no longer hospitable to life.

However, a bizarre contraption in the form of a perfectly hermetic airtight cocoon of safety sealants was found to contain six nearly frozen bodies of the crew and one passenger.

They were not breathing. And yet, they were alive—like ice that is alive—suspended in a strange coma state. When taken to the Medcenter, they had to be revived slowly over a period of over 47 hours.

When he came to and was questioned, Captain Conrad Ehl was very disoriented for days, and claimed irrationally that he had "died" and "come back to life."

The other dazed crew members seemed to concur. Only the single passenger, an emaciated tall woman with a bizarre condition wherein her skin gathered in loose copious folds around her sticklike form—as though it had only recently served to cover a much larger surface perimeter—a so-called Oracle, remained in control, calm and perfectly silent, never offering even that much information.

A week later, upon her recovery from the stasis-like freeze, but her dermal layer still rolling in folds about her, the Oracle made an unusual request. She asked to see "Wisahkh," to see the murky planet surface.

Was she fearless, considered her nurses, or maybe even senseless in asking such a thing after her ordeal? Was this how it had affected her?

But once again she never explained. For, how to explain something so odd, so remotely inhuman? How to explain that she who knew so well the nature of the passing of time, wanted—and had in fact contrived, for once, for a single moment—to experience control over it? To experience the one thing that could truly affect it.

The true intensity of ice.

MOUNT DRAGON

The man stopped at the base of my lower extremities.

Like a puppet, he lowered himself in the crevice between my index stone claw and the slab of granite the weight of which held me down to the earth. He put his microscopic upper appendages forward upon my polished gleaming surface, and willed with all his tiny being for me to attend to him.

I decided to humor both of us.

I answered directly into his mind.

"Go to hell, idiot," I said, using an astringent tongue he'd understand. "I am but a monumental slab of granite, and you, mortality, are like one of the droppings of a fairly large corpulent deity—an ephemeral honor I would rather pass me by."

"And yet, you speak to me, mountain," said the mote of humanity. "Why is that?"

I considered that for a moment. The creature had a point.

"I don't know," I replied honestly.

"But I do."

He stood, waiting for me to respond to his taunt, but I was suddenly weary of this whole exchange, and weary of him.

And so, I ignored him, and eventually he went away, seething with impotence at my lack of curiosity.

But the next day, he was back.

"Because," he said, speaking as though our conversation was never interrupted by a sun's journey across the vault of heaven, the moon's slither, and a spillage of a million stars upon the layers of night, "whereas I am but a single droplet, you are a mountain of divine droppings!"

"So what you're saying," I countered, "is that we're all droppings of the gods? Divine excrement? Fecal material?"

"Yes, shit," he said. "Thus, we are fundamentally of a kind. And being similar, it's in our nature to communicate with each other."

"Really? Interesting. Quite philosophical, even. I thought I was merely a mountain."

"Not just a mountain, but Mount Dragon."

"Only because someone had hewn the base of granite into a legendary form and extrapolated the rest by a wild stretch of mortal imagination. After all, there are only the claws."

"A lot can be inferred from claws," said the man.

"Ah, a claw-reader," I said.

"For example," he continued, nonplused, "I know that your true igneous *draconus* form is imprisoned underneath the weight of stones, that you are locked into the mountain itself by strength of an arcane enchantment."

"Is that so?"

But the man stared up at me, and I could tell that his lips had come together in a confident smile. "You pretend ignorance," he said. "And yet, that is but a part of your supernatural bonds. I had come upon the utmost secret of your being through years of my occult studies, through sleepless nights of gazing at the heavens and transforming the nature of that most base of human metals in the furnace of flames. . . . I alone have the key to your freedom!"

"Freedom?" I said. "No need. I am quite comfortable as I am. Besides, what exactly have you seen in the heavens?"

And yet, as I said it, I knew that this was not quite the truth of it. I sensed some kind of quickening, a beginning circulation of energy and awakening of circuits in the very matter around me. . . .

Could it be that this bit of mortality really knew?

But the man threw up his hands suddenly in a dramatic gesture, and pointed them at me. He leaned back his head, closed his eyes, and began to spout gibberish.

"*Mishakh Kortah!*" he cried, "*Mishakh Kortah Ax Owl Nine!*"

"And your point is?" I responded in mild amusement.

But suddenly, and to my utmost surprise, the beginning of a very remote buzz of slow vibration gathered in the core of the mountain that was myself, a low subsonic rumble. . . .

And for a moment I actually believed in this man's magic.

For several minutes he continued to cry out the meaningless words, and to wave his hands about, and there was an expression of sublime ecstatic effort on his face. Meanwhile, the seismic rumble in the earth, the mountain, echoed and resonated to his words.

Finally he gave up. He sat down on the earth right between one of my claws, and he put his head in his hands in despondency.

"I am powerless . . ." he whispered. "Even all my learning does me nothing, for something very elusive still escapes me. The intricate words dance and twist in my lips, and the gathering power urges me to break free, and yet—"

"And yet nothing seems to happen," I finished.

"Exactly!"

I almost felt sorry for him. And indeed, I suddenly wished he really did have the so-called magic force necessary to do whatever it is that he almost began to do to me, that invigorated me so, and made the very land shudder. . . .

Something occurred to me then. "Why don't you try catching those twisting words, and pinning them down in a different manner?" I said. "It seems that your key may be their very elusive dance. . . ."

He jumped up with an explosion of joy. "Yes!" he cried. "That is the truth of it, *draconus!*"

"I am only a mountain."

But he ignored my last statement, and began once again crying out his meaningless syllables, waving his hands about in gestures of what I thought was pathos. Only, this time he varied the sounds slightly, and I felt the resumption of the sympathetic rumble in the landscape around us.

"*Mishakh Kortakh! Mishaaaaah Konta! Mishahn Kontral Ax Ale Nine!*"

And suddenly, something terribly right happened.

I understood his meaningless words. Understood, and remembered.

Mission Control XL9.

The launch code.

It all came together in one perfect sequence. Because as I remembered the prompt, I simultaneously initialized the execution of the command sequence and remembered all the rest of it, and my internal systems came online, starting a cascading reaction of modular interlock and re-initialization.

The rumble of discord climbed into pure on-pitch ultrasound, and before the man could even put his hands to his weak organic auditory organs, the sound disappeared beyond his hearing range into acute silence.

And then around me, the mountain began to fall apart.

"Fly, *draconus!*" the *homo sapiens* exclaimed in exultation, "I set you free!"

And as my tri-engine thrusters came into play, "Warning!" my auto-comm-systems thundered at his auditory decibel level. "Move away within safety of three hundred meters for launch!"

And a tiny auto-subsystem within me, the same one that had been online all these countless centuries, signaled to the main processor that this primitive will not understand the standard warning directive.

"Run far away!" I cried, switching to the same voice that he had gotten used to hearing in his head. "Run for a league and don't look back, for I will uproot the mountain now, and I will have no harm befall you, my friend who has liberated me!"

And as his fleeting tiny figure began to dart rapidly away, I extended my landing gripper pads—reflective metallic claws that shone brightly beneath the radiation of this alien sun—and retracted the landing gear, while at the same time extending the angular hover-wings that would act like atmospheric rotors to clear the immediate area around my bulk in the seconds of pre-launch.

Finally, I folded the wings, and extended myself into an aerodynamic entity of monochrome silver, recessed the bulkhead with its twin eyelet beams, while all around me the granite layers folded and buckled. And then I signaled the initialization of main thrust.

The mountain fell away, and I was airborne, a silver abstract-dragon shape with a tail of white flame, piercing the lower atmosphere, rising like a reversed meteor into eternity. . . .

Somewhere out there was home.

SALMON IN THE DRAIN PIPE

In the sewer, the water was khaki-colored, running slowly like molasses. The large drain pipe emptied outside into the small half-moon lagoon, and stained the sterile silver of the ocean water with thick ocher of the refuse.

The old man stood watching it. He saw the swirling chunks of old waste come flopping up, like miniature boats straining against the delta waters. Kind of pretty, actually.

Nah, they were ugly as hell, but he just liked imagining that they were natural. It gave him a reason to walk the beach and look at this dirty swill coming out of the drain pipe, because that was about as interesting as things ever got.

He liked to imagine those things were really alive, little living squiggling things, pretty-colored. Pretty yellowish, kind of like goldfish.

The ocean shone razor-bright, silvered at the horizon. The sky, pale winter-white. The whole thing came together like two plastic panels of a similar but not identical chromatic hue snapping into each other, with the horizon a clean sterile seam.

The old man stood, shivering a little, squinting into the smeared blur that was the eye of sun. He pulled his green nylon windbreaker tight about his skinny throat, and took great big gulping, scalding-cold breaths of ocean.

Ah, good.

It was good to feel, to taste, to smell the salt spray, to suck it in through the pores, like an old sponge that he was. Nothing much else was there to take in from the ocean.

Nothing there any more.

The old man stepped along slowly, careful to walk around sharp stones or slippery tar balls, his worn sneakers crunching and smearing occasional remnants of petroleum-based decades-old gunk. He was hunched over from the wind that pushed him in the back, pushed him along on his walk, like it did yesterday, and will again tomorrow.

He'll come back here a little earlier tomorrow, when the tide is still high, and the waters swirl like rich cappuccino froth around the polished stones of the delta, and dance around the coffee grounds that come from the drain pipe.

There'll be bottle caps maybe, little silver and red, like tiny man-o-wars. Or blue and red and white swirly brand name ones, that—if you squint well enough—look like tropical fish in the ocean froth. At some point they will all wash away out there somewhere, to join one of the many flotillas of bottle cap refuse that film over the surface of the world's oceans. *Plastic tides,* they call them. He just calls 'em floaty stuff.

And if he's really lucky, he'll see crumpled paper wrappers, whitish like crab shells, and the old newsprint long unreadable, as it floats off into the silver in an illusion of displaced puffer fish from the depths, and is swallowed by the waves.

Greenish bottles would come floating out sometimes, bobbing like miniature dolphins, and those really made his heart jerk with unexpected pleasure. He'd stand by the drain, eyes half shut, waiting for a rounded bottle form to swim by him, clinking softly against another.

But the best prize of all would be to hear things, as he closed his eyes, listening for the old sound in the surf, a sound that was still there deep in him, even after all this time.

A wave would break, a lull, a hush, a roar of incoming swell. And then, somewhere far away, somewhere between hope and memory, he would almost hear the plaintive bark of a seal. . . . Or was it the flapping of wings and sudden cutting squawks of a seagull gaining altitude, a white streak-shadow of motion? Up, up, against the plastic horizon.

And if he kept his eyes shut after that, against all crazy temptation, just maybe he would hear the ghost bumps of living silence against the corroded walls of the drain.

Bump, bump, went the ghosts.

Just at the brink, almost there, one more over the top of the memory. Almost lost in the soft splashing. . . .

There!

And instantly he would be transported back sixty years, *elsewhere,* into a different place of wide open waters, rushing, blasting the silence, as *they* would clamor, swimming upstream to spawn, their gills pulsing with the life force, thick, virile, seething under the churning water's surface.

Ghosts of salmon. Here, of all places, in this crazy wonderful drain pipe.

SCENT OF THE STARS

When your ashes came to rest
in the gently dug hollows
near the roots of the rosebushes,
when the sky water seeped below,
dissolving the minerals and feeding
the eager green
with the atomic essence,

little did you know
that you would rise with the nutrients
through the firm, crisp stalks and the pliant leaves,
past the buds into the buttery soft rose petals
to become perfume.

And then, once airborne,
fragrant molecules swept into the high atmosphere
over the mountain peaks,
above the cirrus clouds
into the rarified ozone heights,
beyond the chromatic boundary,
bleeding edge of milk-white into cosmic-indigo,

little did you know
that you will continue to soar
with neutrinos, nameless particles, and photons of light
through the endless expanse and the dark matter,
and whatever else undiscovered that pulses in the void,
to become the perfume of the stars.

But maybe you know.
Even now, the universe keeps your scent.

for my father

THE CLOCK KING AND THE QUEEN OF THE HOURGLASS

— 1 —

The Hourglass

Her reason for existence was to become the Queen of the Hourglass.

Liaei was formed from the purest ancient genetic material preserved by the horticulturists, from the largest most succulent ovum of a batch of millions, and from one of the liveliest vector-driven spermatozoa of trillion. Following countless failures, both gametes were filtered and isolated in a superselection process, guaranteeing down to a near-infinite degree of certainty the viability of the combined DNA.

After the egg and sperm were joined in a drop of liquid, the bundle of quickly multiplying cells that was to be Liaei was incubated for the traditional six months under warm golden lights in the nursery, submerged in amber life fluid. The embryo became a delicate pastel bundle of flesh, and then a perfectly formed infant. Microscopic tubes supplied liquid and serum-based nutrients, feeding her while the heart and lungs developed, blood vessels branched out and other organs grew and took on the final female configuration.

On the last day before birth, Liaei floated in the life fluid and was observed with wonder by a room full of darkly golden skinned human and dull metallic machine horticulturists through the glass of her three-tier womb. Amhama, the nurse whose charge Liaei would be, gazed at the perfect child. There were no words. She wiped tears from her dark cheeks with the back of her thin hand and tried to imagine that the fluttering in her lower stomach was merely nerves and not the most sacred and most ancient of human emotions called love.

And yet, it was motherly love that Amhama felt, a strange abstraction, and knowing it she prayed in silence, sending up great soul cries to the bright Day God in gratitude for the honor that had fallen to her.

The voice harmonic echoed meaningless numerics from the natal system. "Thirteen baktun, zero katun, zero tun, zero uinal, zero kin. Time to give birth."

"Go on," said the chief nurse Riveli to Amhama. "Do the honors, Amhama."

Riveli stood back, motioning to the others also, and they crowded away in respect, the combined sheen of their surfaces—golden human skin, pastel organic cloth, and grey machine metal alloy—blending in a soft curvilinear mosaic. Outside the large transparent windows the Day God filled the sky with orange light, and it was the apex of noon. Serendipity or eon-shaped intent, it signified an event of singular importance.

Amhama alone remained standing before the glass womb. She was a frail, gently fading woman with smooth gold skin wrinkling into delicate time-etchings around her egg-shaped face. The sterile natural fiber nursery robe of brilliant white fell in soft listlessness to cover her shallow spots of breasts and torso, wrapping around her thin hips and ending in weightless folds about her bony golden knees.

All smooth, aging, hairless, sterile.

A true mother, she stood.

Amhama lifted her hands to the womb's rotund cover, pressed the release of the first tier, then the second and third, like a falling away of taut onion skins, and finally lifted the inner cover glass for the first time since the incubation six months ago. Slightly arid, sterile nursery air rushed in to disturb the perfect balance of humidity inside the womb, while the infant floating upon the amber liquid sensed the difference and began to stir. Amhama reached inside and started to remove the delicate cobweb of tubing, and with each tug the child squirmed, not so much in pain or discomfort but in surprise.

The final surprise of parting came when the largest central tube was retracted and its thickest portion detached from the navel—a mechanical umbilical cord.

Liaei was now completely separated from the womb, and in the world. Air came into her stimulated lungs and filled her, and pain entered through her navel, and she cried, high pitched agonized, overwhelmed innocent.

She was born.

Amhama gently supported her head and lifted Liaei from the liquefied amber. It ran in rivulets down the newborn's pale delicate surfaces, dripping back into the womb basin, and splattered on Amhama's clothing.

Liaei screamed as she was wrapped in brilliant white sterile fiber.

Parted from the birth ocean, she was completely alone.

At the bottom of the Pacific Basin, a mere rock's toss from the dark lapping waters of the great shallow lake that was all that was left of the Oceanus, huddled the Basin City. It was like a film of mineral deposit at the Oceanus's edges, rimming it, a growth of crystalline structures that in places emerged out of the thick waters like stalagmites, and in others were formed from the clays and rock of the ancient marine sediment that lined the surface of the Basin.

Colors were all tertiary—mauve, teal, dull ocher brown, rich sienna, pale cream, honey amber, salmon clay. Interspersed were patches of gray and ebony rock formations, and chalk-dusted earth. The Basin City structures stood out like islands of chromatic uniformity, impositions of strange, unnatural sterile order. Buildings were placed in rows to approximate city blocks, and streets were upraised platforms of artificial alloy, separated from the unreliable floor sediment that underwent liquefaction so frequently that it was impossible to build upon. Closer to the water's edge, and in some places jutting brazenly into the Oceanus, were grim water refinery plants, domes of concrete and steel surrounded with bands of metal scaffolding and pipes that siphoned off the super-saturated salt sludge-water into appropriate reservoirs for processing. Here the toxic blood of the Oceanus was vaporized, then returned back to liquid state, and captured in post-processing reservoirs that delivered distilled water to the whole of Basin City and beyond. Pipes and tubes ran off in all directions below and above the sediment ground. Some of the water was redirected into local aqueducts that rested on thick columns fifty meters in height and covered with transparent plasti-glass on the topside to prevent evaporation into the thin arid atmosphere.

Finally, the largest thickest post-processing waterpipe, with the diameter of a small canal, fed directly from the tallest processing dome and ran through the heart of Basin City and out and up the Basin slope.

It was said that it had been originally built thousands of years ago with enough clay and concrete and metal alloy to reach the halfway point of the slope walls of the Pacific Basin, and then for some reason the project was abandoned. Looking back, some thought the building materials had run out. Others supposed it was lack of interest or funding. Whatever the reason, the high-tech civilization of the time did not complete the building of the waterline pipe all the way up the Pacific Basin walls. But instead of abandoning the water delivery project completely, a marvelous impossible technology was used to continue to channel the water up the Basin slope without the pipe.

The water was made to run uphill, never touching the ground, suspended through the air.

Amhama liked to smile and talk to the child Liaei. As the girl grew human and the woman grew older, the bond between them was formed with words.

"Liii-aaah-eeeh-iiih," Amhama sang in a breathy voice, leaning over the crib. The light came amber-sweet from the window, coloring Amhama's smooth forehead and hairless scalp, coloring the infant's face, overflowing into the room, and the distant heavy indigo shape of the Oceanus defined the horizon. Above and beyond stretched the great slope of the Basin—no sky was visible from the vantage point of the window, only remote Basin walls that loomed like golden shadows of slate, and desiccated dust sweeping bedrock in the haze-filled background. The Basin gathered the intense light from the sky and kept it, pooling inward where it reflected off the walls and colored the air golden. The surface of the Oceanus shimmered, the film over its thick waters iridescent like benzene, undulating with temporary rainbows and then again dark.

Amhama moved her gaze farther outward, narrowed her eyes to better focus, and saw the pale white speck of a ship sailing out into the heart of the waters. "Look," she whispered, knowing that Liaei was too young to respond or be aware, but wanting to speak nevertheless. "There goes a white ship! A great voyager, a brave explorer! Imagine how fearless, how insolent, to skim along the treacherous surface of the Oceanus."

Liaei stared back, great jewel eyes glistening with moisture and of indeterminate hue.

"That's right, the fearless ship sails!" said Amhama again. "It will never come back, probably. Fearless white ship! Silly, silly ship that will sink in toxic salt."

And then she laughed and drew her fingers along the child's soft cheek and the amazing growth of pale white-gold hair that started from above her forehead. "You are safe here, my sweet-eyes. Unlike the ship, you are here with me, and you are safe."

Liaei looked back with wide eyes at her nurse and voluntary mother. And she looked through her, maybe. Because her infant eyes did not focus or see—not yet.

When Liaei was five, she jumped and danced like a creature of fluid and no bones or flesh—flexible and malleable like a jellyfish, resilient and light like the bouncing ball she played with. "Ama! Ama!" she sang as she moved seemingly nonstop around the rooms, galloping barefoot through their apartment. And Amhama answered fondly with "Liii-aaah-eeeh-iiih!" as she went about her own chores.

Each night Amhama left the child sleeping as she rose and got dressed in the deepest period of darkness and left their apartment to work her shift at the medicineal. She walked along the winding upraised streets illuminated softly with transparent lanterns, with absolute darkness pressing in from above, the sky and Basin a kettle of ink. There was no need to take a transport, since the walk was less than ten blocks along the largest street of Basin City. The lantern light dispelled the night and made it safe. And the patrolling police cars swept along frequently, hovering without a sound, their vaguely oval shapes skimming the air at street level. One of the cars had its security plasti-glass top down and an officer—familiar to Amhama because they nearly always seemed to share this shift—waved to her and then was on his way.

Amhama smiled and waved back, then drew her street jacket closer against the night's dry chill breeze, and hurried, so as not to be late. The medicineal building was one of the tallest structures in Basin City, a tower of several hundred floors, and it loomed before her. Once inside, she entered the first sterilization floor, was cleansed and then proceeded in a lift to the two hundredth floor in the horticulturist section, where she worked with other growers of mammal embryos to produce human gametes. Amhama was one of the specialists with the highest experience in genetics and was thus often assigned to special case homo sapiens. Elsewhere in the building, the horticulturists developed other very occasional animal species and mostly plantlife DNA and created hybrids that were brought to hothouse maturation. Here, in the Special Projects section, were the unusual select projects, such as Liaei. Indeed, it was so easy to forget that Liaei was Amhama's project, a unique responsibility, and not merely a beloved child.

"How is she?" Chief nurse Riveli asked Amhama every time as Amhama came to the section desk to begin her shift. There was never a need to clarify whom Riveli meant.

"Sleeping well tonight," Amhama replied with an involuntary smile. "I gave her a kiss and she did not even stir as she usually does. I fed her the thick protein and melatonin-enriched cocktail before bedtime, and it seems to be calming her down enough to allow her to sleep within the hour of lying down. Otherwise she is still unstoppable."

"You are rather unstoppable yourself," replied Riveli, smiling widely, without looking up from the work display on her desk. "No one else in our section would have dared to do this thing, you know. To singlehandedly raise the Queen of the Hourglass."

"Ah, she is just my Liaei," said Amhama. "Not a Queen of anything yet."

Riveli looked up, and for a moment there was a pitying expression in her steady eyes. "She is what she is, Amhama. Since the moment of fertilization. You know it since you put her cells together. She may seem an ordinary child, even though hyperactive, but soon enough the differences will become prominent. Her energy levels alone are but precursors."

"Oh, I know," said Amhama, and as though remembering, ran her hands down her own slender undifferentiated body, the line of her waist and hips completely lacking concavity. "It is just a nice way of talking about her now, while I still may."

"Forgive me for being blunt as always," said Riveli. "I just don't want you to get hurt from yearning."

But Amhama unfolded her sterile white robe and was putting it on, and had turned her back to Riveli.

The following year, Liaei had reached formal learning age, and she now accompanied Amhama to the medicineal every morning. To accommodate Liaei's fragile sleeping schedule, Amhama had taken a later shift, and now worked starting an hour after dawn. They walked together in the dawning hours, the child Liaei harnessed to Amhama with a short safety leash just in case, even though they held hands. The air was cool and crisp with dryness, with occasional slightly noxious and humid gusts from the Oceanus reaching them here many meters away. The moisture was ephemeral however, for it immediately dispersed upon the wind and more often it was an arid breeze that swept along the surface of the skin. They watched the sky that started high above at the distant lofty edges of the Basin walls take on color. First, it paled from darkness into silver, then, as the Day God rose and engulfed all overhead, it became sudden flaming amber and the Basin was filled with light.

Dawns came sudden in the Basin.

"Look!" Amhama would say, pointing to a sudden flaring speck of brightness, a hair-line ribbon of light that began halfway up the Basin slope and culminated at the high edges.

"The River!" Liaei said, bounding along at her side, clutching Amhama's larger dry hand in her soft moist own.

"The River That Flows Through The Air!" said Amhama. "Isn't it wonderful and bright? We can see it all the way from here, when it is so far away. Kilometers upon kilometers."

"Why is it so bright, Ama?" Liaei asked, while the dawn wind stirred her hair into brightness also. "Is it made from light?"

"No, it's water, silly. When the Day God shines upon clean transparent water, its light reflects back into your eyes and mine. The Oceanus would be shiny too, but it is so thick with salt and chemicals that the light does not reflect the same way."

"Is that why the Oceanus is so dark always? I hate it, it is creepy," said Liaei.

"The Oceanus is nasty, but at the same time it is wonderful, because that's where the last of our water comes from. Nowhere on our Earth is there any more water left, only here. That's why we live here."

But Liaei continued to stare at the thin distant ribbon of light on the Basin slope. "I want to see the River," she said softly.

Amhama sighed. "You will, child, soon enough. There's another city up there, on the very top. Just beyond where the River flows into the horizon and disappears. One day you will go there."

"I want to see the River *now*." There was a whiny tone to Liaei's normally musical voice. "Please!"

"Well, we can't. I need to work and you have class. And the way there is just too long and difficult and uncomfortable, and besides we can't afford it."

Liaei tugged at Amhama's hand, and then frowned so that her whole little face contorted like a soft malleable thing. Her dark gold eyebrows shaped evenly with follicles of natural hair swept upward at the inner edges, then down, lending expressiveness to her face that was already so much more defined than Amhama's own. Compared to her, Amhama was a smooth egg-headed doll with generic even features and only warm eyes that added individuality. But unlike Liaei, Amhama's eyes were infinitely tired, it seemed, tired in essence, in their origin.

The girl did not seem to notice it or understand the nature of this tiredness, and continued to pull at the woman's hand periodically, all the while repeating, "Ama, I want to see the

River, please, oh please, can we go see the River, Ama, oh please!" She whined and stomped her feet with forcefulness so that her light sandals made a clatter against the dull alloy surface of the street. She jumped up and down and then leaned down in a crouch and tried to drag Amhama's hand to her level.

"No!" said Amhama finally, tightening her hold on the small moist living hand, and pulled her along, almost with regret, as they turned the final block to the medicineal building. "Not now, Liaei, not now. Stop that, girl! I have to work. Understand? And you have to study."

Liaei began to wail, her six-year old lungs grasping the arid air, and then suddenly stopped. She saw a multicar passing by, the standard Basin City school transport. Amhama watched Liaei as she stared at the many smooth hairless heads of the other children visible through the plasti-glass, their faces even-featured and similar to each other, their skins of all golden shades from light to dark. Liaei was mesmerized.

It was a wrenching feeling Amhama got every time she saw Liaei like that. Liaei wanted to be there in that multicar with the other children, wanted to attend the ordinary public school. And although it had been explained to her by both Amhama and Riveli with careful gentle tact, Amhama knew that Liaei stifled inside of her a rebellious intensity and did not believe their reasons for keeping her separate were good enough.

The school transport moved past them and down the street. Its hover path was swept clean of dust, leaving the surface of the road dark in the place where it had been. Liaei stood staring in its wake, watching it disappear beyond the curve of the street. She had grown silent, forgetting that only a moment ago she had been struggling and almost crying. The grip of her fingers had loosened in Amhama's own. She walked in numb obedience at Amhama's side and did not speak another word as they entered the medicineal building.

"You have old DNA," Amhama had explained to Liaei that day as they sat in a sterile metallic office on the 204th floor together with Riveli. Riveli's smooth even-featured face was almost like Amhama's and her skin was only a few shades of darker gold. The difference was, Riveli watched the child seated on a chair before them with her expression blank, and her smile seemed pasted on for lack of true involvement. She watched Liaei as though she were a clinical specimen—which she was—watched her initial fidgeting and mobility, observed it change into malleable silence and seriousness, the whole transition mercurial and impossibly alive.

"Old DNA means that your genetic makeup is almost original to the ancient homo sapiens species, and not a tapering off post-hybrid like most of the rest of us," said Amhama kindly. "It means that you are special and your life force and will and developmental potential is very very strong."

"Do you understand what that means, Liaei?" asked Riveli.

Amhama, uncomfortable with the girl's continued silence, went on. "You know how I always get tired, Liaei? And how you almost never seem to be tired, and want to move around so much so that I scold you constantly? Well, to be honest, sweetheart, I have no right to tell you to stop moving so much, since this is part of what makes you so very special. I am the one who is dull and slow, compared to you."

"You are not dull, Ama," blurted Liaei suddenly. "And I don't want to be special. I want to be like you."

Riveli sighed.

Amhama moved her lips, tightened them.

"I don't want old DNA," continued Liaei. "Why must I have it? Can you take it away?"

Amhama opened her mouth to speak, but Riveli raised her hand to stop her, and then said, "What you have, child, is what everyone in the world right now would give everything to have. You were made with the best of what we have left. The strongest, cleanest of defect, most likely to survive. We made you that way so that you would do great wonderful things for the remainder of the human species."

"Why?" said Liaei, staring somewhere between Riveli's chin and her thin neck.

"Don't you want to help all of us?" persisted Riveli, and her pasted on smile did not waver. Amhama wanted to wipe that smile off her face with a swipe of her fingers.

"I want to be just like everyone else . . ." replied Liaei. She was beginning to frown, and a stormy expression was gathering which Amhama knew so well. And so, to distract the oncoming tempest, she brought up that thing for the first time, the thing which sat like a rock in her innards.

"Why would you want to be like everyone else, boring and ordinary, when you are going to be the Queen of the Hourglass?"

"Amhama!" said Riveli, her gaze coming into focus with alarm. "No, she is too young."

"Not too young to start learning," retorted Amhama. "At least some of it."

Liaei's frown relaxed and she was immediately mesmerized. "What is the Queen of the Hourglass, Ama?" she said in a completely different tone, forgetting her complaints.

Amhama smiled, then laughed. "The Queen of the Hourglass!" she said in her familiar sing-song tone. "The Queen of the Hourglass is a most wonderful thing to be! That's you, Liaei! But first you must go to your class, and behave, and after that I promise I will tell you more."

When Liaei had her mind set on something, she became focused and intensely driven. That day Liaei paid precise, almost unhealthy attention to her lessons from the edu-system voice harmonic—as Amhama discovered when she ran the child's regular progress report—and when they returned home after eating dinner at the medicineal building cafeteria, Amhama saw how Liaei was unusually subdued, biting her lips and looking at a point before her, paying no attention to anything around them. She wanted so badly to ask her, Amhama knew, and yet, something held her back.

It was as though the child was afraid of hearing the answer. Twilight gathered over Basin City in ephemeral rolling mists that would fade even before full night came, dissipating into arid darkness, when Liaei finally came up to Amhama who sat, fingers moving lightly, reading the dots from her armchair display. She tapped her arm and said, "Ama."

Amhama looked up to see the earnest eyes, the dark golden brows and curls forming over a smoothly curving oval face, frozen in intensity like a doll, a peculiar mechanical creature. Liaei was so living that she seemed unreal. Her facial muscles were microscopic and perfect in their organization.

"The Queen of the Hourglass," she said. "Tell me."

Amhama bit her own lip. And then, thinking in a tumult, she said, "Let me show you." Amhama turned the reading display so that both of them could see the rows of raised reading dots impressed in the slowly turning drum. Then she thought for a moment, put her fingers on the switch to stop the drum rotation and called up a search on the harmonium pad. "Search Hourglass," she told the machine.

And instants later the search came tumbling back at them. "The Hourglass," said the harmonium at the same time as the drum turned, "is an ancient device to measure the passing of an abstract construct called time. It postdates the sundial, predates the clock and the computer and the harmonium."

Amhama watched Liaei's face.

"I don't understand," said the girl, why would anyone measure the passing of time? I thought time just is? And what are all those things it mentioned?"

"Ancient machines," replied Amhama. "The closest predecessors of the harmonium systems were these things called computers that relied on the fluctuation of an energy called electricity that had something to do with the magnetic poles of the earth, I think. Or maybe it's a type of solar radiation? A bit of it's what's in those weak static fields that sometimes can be detected by the harmonium. Though, I am not sure, since much of this information has been lost with the same civilization that had built the River That Flows Through The Air."

For a moment Liaei's expression lightened, as Amhama imagined she was distracted by the pleasant memory of Day God's dayfire reflected upon a thread of white flame along the Basin slope. Liaei really loved the River, loved hearing about it, seeing it every day as they walked outside. Someday they must visit, but now, there was this to deal with.

"So anyway, there was this energy source that ran all that technology that no longer functions. All those weird machine relic carcasses that people sometimes find buried along the Basin walls or even up there on the Plateau beyond. They say there are ancient cities there, covering the surface of the earth with their sad rubble, all useless parts and objects that once meant a great deal but now there isn't even a memory of their function. They just lie there, overgrown with drybrush cacti and half-covered with sand."

"The Hourglass . . ." whispered Liaei, interrupting Amhama gently.

"Oh yes. Sorry, let's ask it some more, let's see what it says about that."

They asked what the hourglass looked like and how it worked. "A sealed glass container of specific cubic volume separated into two equal parts by a slim tube neck with an opening of a certain width and one part filled with just enough granules of sand or other powdered material to mark the passage of a specific period of time," the harmonic voice told them. "It is turned repeatedly so that the powder runs from one side to the other through the narrow opening."

"How weird and useless!" said Liaei.

"But it was not useless, back in those ancient times, sweet," said Amhama. "People used it to keep track of their daily activity, their lives. They didn't know about the clockwork mechanism just yet, did not know about interlocking gears and counterweights and pulleys, so they had to use this simple device."

"What about the Queen?" said Liaei.

"That's another story for another day."

Amhama had the rare ability to stall—not just for days and weeks but for months and years. Amhama dropped tiny snippets of new information about the Queen, and Liaei continued to ask relentlessly, so that in a sense they tortured each other constantly without getting anywhere.

Liaei grew very quickly, grew tall and filled out with softness, and was now fourteen years old. There was a bountiful layer of pale golden hair growing from Liaei's scalp, and it now reached below her waist. Amhama, her own scalp bare as everyone else's, helped Liaei cut it many times, touching the soft strands in wonder, amazed at the profusion of this energy. She traced the brow hair at the ridge above Liaei's golden-green eyes, and marveled at the spikes of lashes fringing the eyes—for Amhama had none of her own.

Liaei's slender long-limbed body had also taken on strange prominent curves, hips expanding and waist tightening, and the breasts budding at first with sharp tips and then swelling with roundness that was so alien compared to Amhama's own flat chest.

"What is happening to me?" asked Liaei often. She also asked the harmonium so many variations of questions about the Queen of the Hourglass that she knew now for a fact that the Queen was a creature made to perform a single very important function, and that had something to do with the Clock King— another creature similar to herself yet specialized in a different way.

"You are growing," replied Amhama, smiling gently. Liaei was used to the ambiguity of that smile, unsure whether it contained sorrow or pleasure or a mixture of both and something else altogether.

"So I am to be the mate of this Clock King," said Liaei, a statement of fact, for she no longer asked Amhama things as much as she restated what she learned on her own. Even her voice was deep and mellifluous now, unlike Amhama's somewhat childish androgynous timbre.

"Yes."

"Is that why my body is so animalistic?"

Amhama sighed. "Must you call it so? It is simply the body of a younger human race with a different level of hormonal development."

It was fascinating how fluid was the movement of Liaei's face, the dance of her brows that reflected every emotion. Compared to her, Amhama was a mechanized puppet with a limited set of facial movements. Even now, Liaei's facial muscles fluttered, expressing anger, a suppressed violent mystery of some emotion alien to Amhama. And her eyes—the intensity was painful to observe.

"Yes, animalistic," said Liaei. "What else would you call this? I am fertile and disgusting, and soon—any day now—will bleed on a regular basis. Yes, the harmonium told me thoroughly what you and the medicineal have been trying to keep from me so carefully. All the while as you watch me, and record every tiny new thing. Apparently I am almost ready to begin the full Queen training. It has to do with my interaction with the Clock King."

Liaei got up from the seat before Amhama. She moved about the room with a grace and speed, so that the finely woven fiber material of her clothing seemed to lag behind her in delayed motion, sweeping around her curves as though driven by an invisible wind. Liaei came to the window of their apartment, the same window from which she had stared for the past fourteen years, and the Day God shone brightly outside, reflecting against the inky darkness of the Oceanus in the distance. It, the great lake, had receded inward even more within those fourteen years, so that the black water that had lapped at the edges of the shore at the refineries when Liaei was born, was now about a meter away, revealing more crystalline rock and sediment at the rim.

Amhama watched Liaei's form as she stood illuminated by the brilliant dayfire, watched her curving profile, the parabolic lines. "Ama," said Liaei, not turning her head. "How long do I have, before I am Queen?"

Amhama was still, even her breath falling off.

"Ama!" said Liaei, turning suddenly to face her almost-mother. "Please tell me! I'd rather hear it from you than the harmonium."

"Two more years."

The words came reluctant, slow. For in that moment Amhama did not want to speak at all, wanted to postpone, to delay, to put off forever. Words always seemed to speed up the course of events. Words made them concrete and inevitable.

Liaei took several steps and then came down in a crouch before the seated woman and put her hand on Amhama's golden skin, her forearm. Her palms were moist and warm. She looked into Amhama's motionless tired eyes.

"And when will I begin the training?"

There was a breeze that blew in the open window, and it carried a moist and queasy scent of Oceanus. Liaei's face wrinkled in involuntary revulsion from the toxicity, and in that moment it occurred to Amhama how sensitive, how fragile she was, this growing child. Her child and yet not hers. How ephemeral.

"I'll talk to Riveli," said Amhama. "Tomorrow."

Neither Riveli nor Amhama had changed much over the fourteen years. Liaei saw Riveli on a regular basis, every several months, for various interviews, physical and psychological tests, and at every sign of developmental change.

Riveli always remained neutral, showing as little emotion as possible, even less so than was normal. Amhama told Liaei that it was her way of maintaining professional distance, but Liaei had the distinct impression Riveli did not like her, even resented her progress over the years. But Riveli and Amhama were two main individuals of the few people Liaei interacted with, since she was never enrolled in a regular school. Other children Liaei's age grew into poised androgynous teens and she saw them in passing on the streets, in the apartment complex where they lived, in the transport vehicles along roadways, at the food centers and general stores. They were young smooth aliens.

But Riveli was a comfort in her predictability, and Liaei knew what to expect.

"We'll start the training this week," said Riveli, watching her desk display as she nearly always did, not looking at Liaei directly. "Most of the training will involve reading material, and the harmonium will provide it. Some of it will be physical exercises—since you will have to maintain absolute muscle tone and precision in addition to proper hormone levels. A horticulturist tech pair will work with you."

"And all of my progress will be measured and recorded."

Riveli glanced briefly in the girl's direction. "That is correct."

Liaei nodded. She then wrinkled her nose.

"A Queen rules at the side of the King, as his consort," said the harmonium. "In a matriarchal society the Queen has the primary power, while in a patriarchal society, it is the King."

"What about our society?" asked Liaei. She was seated before her display in the classroom cubicle of the medicineal, a tiny room beneath a directed skylight that had been set up specifically for her, and the harmonium adjusted to interact with her voice at all levels of knowledge. The display consisted of the slowly turning plasti-alloy drum frame covered like a sieve with dotholes at specific intervals. As the drum turned with inner mechanical clockwork, rounded pins entered and receded from the dot holes in various combinations of semantic code, and Liaei observed them and derived meaning. Once she had had to keep her fingertips upon the dots but now it had become second nature, so all she needed was to look. The drum simply turned at individual rates, as needed, and Liaei's drum moved faster than anyone's, because she was a natural speed reader.

The voice option was also enabled, so that Liaei heard what she was reading spoken by a synthetic machine voice. And occasionally, there would be a fluid sparkle and crackle of static as the small rectangle above the drum lit up with the strange energy that was neither particle nor wave, and it would display still or moving images to better illustrate the textual material.

"Our society is a multicracy based on resource allocation. The sexes are limited in function, so the allocation of power along such lines is irrelevant. Thus, the King and the Queen are ritualized roles and their influence upon our society is only in a very specific area. They do not rule in the ancient traditional sense."

"So what do they do?" said Liaei, a mixture of frustrated curiosity and tension evident in her voice and in the way she leaned forward and fingered the smooth edge of the quickly turning drum.

Unlike a human being, the harmonium never hesitated when presented with a clear question. It replied, "The Queen of the Hourglass and the Clock King manipulate time."

The Oceanus was a blotch of darkness, a dull spill of crude oil upon the horizon of the Basin. It was an overcast morning and the Day God was hidden beyond a layer of whisper-thin airborne precipitate—a most unusual sight in any season, but now it was winter. Liaei wore a thick windbreaker garment with a hood, ankle-high water-impermeable boots, and thermal pants. And yet she shivered because her face was open to the wind. It was a spot of absolute cold on her otherwise climate-controlled body.

"Almost done, only another two hundred meters," spoke the childlike machine voice of the horticulturist tech moving smoothly behind her along the crumbling rocks of the shoreline. Liaei took careful footholds, for the sediment closest the water was frozen in places with a fine paper-thin layer of slippery ice, dull gray and impure like the water itself. It was so fine that it crumbled at the slightest pressure, but even so, one had to walk carefully. The Oceanus never froze over because of its chemical content, but the proximity of moisture created that strange dirty semi-rime on the shore.

Liaei's daily walk was made difficult today by the wind pressure. She glanced occasionally at the Basin slope beyond the City but there was no sky brilliance to tell her where on the slope lay the thread that was The River That Flows Through The Air—there was only the overcast. The Basin walls rose in increasing darkness from all directions, and the rust and earth-tone colors of the rock were supplanted by the monochrome gray.

About a hundred meters in the distance, along the shoreline was a dark silhouette of a human figure. As Liaei made her way toward it, the figure waved, and with proximity the shape resolved itself into Toliwe the human tech, also assigned to work with her. Toliwe was only a little older than Liaei, but he was one of the most advanced horticultural interns at the medicineal.

Toliwe stood immobile, waiting for her. His gauntness was obscured by the thick windbreaker garments, and the dark seared-gold patch of skin that was his face was impenetrable from the distance.

Liaei quickened her walk and as soon as she had reached Toliwe's side he silently nodded and matched her stride, falling in line several paces behind her. They were all walking the last hundred meters, strung out among the rocks of the shore, toward the designated mark.

The rock and sediment tapered off, ending at a long artificial pier that formed somewhere inland toward Basin City and protruded out past the sloping shore into the lapping inky thickness of the waters. Here it was suspended on slim columns of concrete that disappeared into the water, and the last few meters it seemed to float.

Liaei was the first to reach the pier. Fleet-footed and light, she almost ran the last few steps, so that angry sand and gravel poured down the remainder of the slope before the pier began. Jumping onto the smooth surface she stood immobile, just as suddenly frozen with intensity, her face turned to the Oceanus wind, full force. Toliwe was a few steps behind, but he lacked her energy as he stepped upon the pier.

"Course completed successfully," said the machine tech behind them, gliding in place. It stood and folded its runners and now unfurled glide-wings from the ovoid surface of its metallic hull. "I'll be on my way, Liaei," it continued. "Great job today, once again. See you tomorrow."

Liaei smiled, even though there was no need, and said, breathless from the chill wind, "Thank you, Mara. Yes, it was great as always, see you!"

"The stats, please?" Toliwe said. His human voice was somehow more machinelike than Mara's. Liaei glanced at him only once and then back again at the dark liquid expanse. She often felt a kind of emotional void in Toliwe's company—not because she did not like him but rather because he was reserved and serious and almost never smiled, never engaged in fake small talk.

"She did very well," Mara said. "With base capacity resting heart rate 72 beats per minute, maximum heart rate 212 bpm, her current heart rate is 131 bpm. Heart rate is not particularly elevated considering the oxygen requirement of her smaller-capacity lungs, and red blood cell levels. This was a brisk walk, nearly a jog, and the windchill factor must be taken into consideration."

Toliwe nodded. "Thank you, Mara. Please forward the results to my lab, including the wind and barometric pressure."

"As always, forwarding now," responded Mara, with more human inflection in the machine voice than his, and with a hint of a vocal smile. And then Mara's glide wings activated, extending on both sides of its chassis, and a near-silent hum of cutting air turbulence was all around them. In seconds Mara rose, was meters above them like an ovoid metal bird, and then hurtled into the sky, on its way back to the medicineal.

Liaei turned from her view of the Oceanus to stare at the receding gray speck of the horticulturist, fading quickly into the overcast.

Toliwe meanwhile took out his recording pad and called up yesterday's data.

"How do you feel, Liaei?" he asked politely, without looking away from his task.

"I'm fine," she replied. "A little cold. I mean, I am warm from the exercise, but the breathing is cold. Hurts a little to inhale when it's windy and cold like this."

"Understandable, since your lung capacity is genetically not optimal for our present atmospheric conditions. Ideally you require about 10 percent more oxygen in the cocktail."

"Yes, me and my primitive lungs." Liaei looked down at the bits of gravel and sand scattered along the edges of the pier where she stood, bits that had fallen from her boots.

Toliwe looked up, his face a mask of fine regular features, androgynous, smooth and deep gold skin, hairless. "Your lungs are perfectly fine, but they would function at optimal capacity in a more oxygen-rich and more humid atmosphere. So you must be careful to exercise at a heightened level to maintain regular tone."

"You sound like the harmonium, do you know?" said Liaei. She glanced at him and for a moment met his eyes—dark and placid and cool in their composure. Studying her as a specimen.

For the first time Toliwe smiled. It was bright, a grin baring perfect white teeth, charming and forceful. Liaei looked away briefly, dazzled.

"Sorry, Liaei, I get carried away with numbers, and thanks for reminding me," he said, his voice taking on a more gentle inflection, his intelligent eyes matching hers. "Now, are you ready for the balance routine?"

Liaei nodded. She then adjusted the laces at her throat that held the hood of her windbreaker, and then pulled, releasing so that it fell back. A strong gust of wind came in that moment, tugging at her ponytail, sending up fine shorter strands in all directions so that they stood up like a fierce static field, while the bulk of her gathered hair flapped against her back.

Toliwe slipped off his own hood, revealing a bare deep golden scalp. He then proceeded to unseal his windbreaker, heedless of the chill factor, folded it neatly, then placed it down on the pier and rested his data pad on top to keep it from being blown away. Underneath he wore only a loose natural fiber short-sleeved t-shirt, and it flapped wildly about his slender perfectly toned torso.

"Keep yours on," he said, seeing that Liaei considered momentarily if she should also take off her windbreaker. "At least for today. It really is too cold for you."

"But I cannot move very well in this."

"You can move well enough."

And with those words he started the routine, and Liaei followed him.

They moved in fluid acrobatic figures, repeating the ancient motions of Fua, the most ancient of hybrid martial defense and philosophy arts. Toliwe breathed lightly, heedless of the freezing gusts that beat at him, and Liaei focused, trying to distance herself from the cold that swept her head, focus on the living breath and inner tranquil balance. She moved like a delicate perfect dancer despite her heavy thick outer clothing, and did not know that her grace matched Toliwe effortlessly, matched his slim androgynous long limbs with her more rounded flexibility. Their movements were precise like repetitive motion of mechanical blades, and yet smooth and organic.

Gentle, yielding, flexible, always in motion to stay in place—the principle of Fua.

The moments stretched into a wind-filled timelessness, and eventually the routine was done.

Toliwe stilled in the final form, with his feet planted together and his hands coming forward with palms meeting each other, then finally falling at his sides. Liaei was in the same moment, moving like his mirror image, and stopped exactly when he did. They stood one opposite the other, wind-beaten statues. Taking three deep breaths they then bowed to one another.

"Well done," said Toliwe, becoming his own remote self, fluidity seeming to pull inward and retreat somewhere deep inside of him, to be replaced with stilted silence. In that moment the Day God broke through the overcast momentarily, filling the gray dimness of the Basin with an outpouring of warm golden light.

Liaei looked up to see the spider-thin string of light rising from the midpoint of the Basin slope, like a single blazing hair fallen from the head of the Day God. She smiled involuntarily and then met Toliwe's gaze.

Toliwe watched her, his dark eyes steady, and again she could not read the depth of his expression. Finally he looked away and went to retrieve his windbreaker and data pad. He observed the small recording drum turning rapidly, and the simultaneous output of the raised dot code, then the harmonium image diagram that arose like a film of invisible energy above the pad within the containing rectangle window.

Liaei released a breath she did not know she had been holding, and once again looked at the distant thread of light that was The River That Flows Through The Air.

"Your body has nearly achieved menarche," said the harmonium, "and your hormone production is surging. Very soon the levels will be at their peak, at which point you will be ready to perform as the Queen of the Hourglass."

"I am to copulate with the Clock King," responded Liaei. "Yes I know. But to what end? Will my body actually become a viable reproduction mechanism, as it had been in the ancient times? Am I to bear human offspring, is that it? What good will it do for the bulk of humanity, our basically asexual, functionally sterile modern homo sapiens, for me to bear one or two children the ancient way? A replenishing of the dying gene pool? Am I not an anachronism already and not viably integrateable with this pretty much different human species?"

"These are all rhetorical questions, or do you want me to answer them?"

Liaei grimaced. "Answer, please. All of them."

"Liaei, your role is vital. Not only are you going to mate and procreate, but you and your offspring will be integrated into the current gene pool in order to invigorate it. Despite what it might seem, your material is still close enough to be genetically homogenized. Even if you bear one offspring only, it should be sufficient, and no one is expecting for you to become the new Eva."

Liaei snorted, recalling the ancient story of the first woman and man. "It's funny," she said to herself in a soft voice, "how the sophisticated ancient technologies that once ruled the world fade from memory and record but simple ancient stories like this one remain, passed on by word of mouth. But then, it probably comes down to the nature of simplicity, the rule of the ordinary. Doesn't it?"

But the harmonium continued, ignoring her aside. "Creating the Queen from the ancient DNA is a meticulous and difficult task, and with each generation it becomes more difficult due to the dearth of preserved viable material to work with. It is not a well-publicized fact, but in the process of matching the numerous gamete pairs to form you, we have likely depleted the stores of ancient genetic material. You therefore, are possibly not the first woman of your kind but the last."

"Great, that really makes me feel better," said Liaei. "Why couldn't you make a whole bunch of Queens? I find it hard to believe that there were not enough ova and sperm cloning material for more than just me."

The harmonium was momentarily silent. And then it said, "We tried. But we could not. True, there was plenty of genetic material in the stores, preserved for thousands of years in pristine cryo-condition. But your pair was the only one that became fertilized after several thousand attempts. The rest simply died. As you see, Liaei, the true reason you are so special is because in the past thirteen decades you are the only one who lived."

Liaei danced. The door to her room was locked for privacy and to shut out the sound. She knew that on the other side, Amhama was reading in the living room, trying to ignore the pulsing base vibrations that came from the sound system. Ever since Liaei discovered that her body enjoyed moving quickly and in rhythm, and that there were certain types of music that made her excited and breathless and wanting to whirl and jump in time, heedless of actual physical form or control, unlike the precision of Fua—ever since, Liaei made it a habit to lock herself away and call up the wildest, usually ancient music from the archives. Fua was just not enough. Other young people like Toliwe and some of the other horticulturists at the medicineal, gathered together to listen to melodious complex soundfests, attended concerts, pub-clubs, and would often get up and move in rhythm also, but soft, fluid, stately—completely Fua in its nature. Modern music was all like that, even the beat remote and barely supporting the melody, like an afterthought. Beat, rhythm, time, was never emphasized. Grace and continuity was what drove them, what captured their imagination and physical need.

But Liaei needed something more. "I am the Queen of the Hourglass, whatever that really means," she thought, "and damn it, but I enjoy time, enjoy its manifestation in the continuity and intervality of human-made melodic sound. Time is the cessation and resumption of movement. Just like music, time is binary, on-off. It is a thing of complexity and energy bound inextricably into one. Modern music just does not have the same energy that I need. It may be enough for them. But I am an anachronism, and I will unabashedly enjoy anachronistic things that resonate within me."

And so Liaei danced, locked away in her room, with the shades drawn over the one window. She had asked the harmonium to synchronize the indoor illumination with the pulse of sound it generated in the audio projectors, and the room was filled with the breath of sound and the sway of tertiary color hues—rose, mauve, rust, sienna, teal, heliotrope.

The sound of ancient instruments preserved for millions of years was terrifying in its beauty and remoteness, the raw essence spanning time. There were instruments that created sound by means of air passing through narrow enclosures, instruments of the wind. There were others, based on friction, the sound of ancient hair follicles of extinct animals rubbing against taut strings of artificial and natural substances for which there were no longer any definitions. Finally, there were the instruments of percussion, resulting in sound based on the striking of hard surfaces against other variable surfaces of various texture and tension. When it all came together in peculiar smooth harmony, syncopation, shattered with instants of dissonance, it was like coming home. Time splintered, blended, streamed, heightened in tension and then resolved.

And Liaei moved with it.

Liaei swayed, her hands moving in waves that began at her fingertips and ended at her shoulders, all of her body fluid, malleable. Her torso and waist were the center of warmth, radiating outward, and the muscles of her legs were springs of living clockwork, chaotic, random and yet precise, blending their movement with the outpouring of sound. She spun around the center of herself, the burning heart of the spindle, and her long loosened hair flew in a curtain.

The music was a wild feast of whistle-notes and rich rolling vibrato of strings, the soaring of the many played as one, the clangor of ethereal reverberation and the thunder of the drums. The sound made all the tiny hairs on her body stand on end, and her nerve endings buzzed with exultation.

And there were occasional recordings that contained on them human voices. They were glorious and alien, for they had come from the deepest antiquity, and they rang in the here and now like ghosts of the original humanity.

Liaei internalized the plurality of sound, moving faster or slower according to the rhythm that drove it all. And as she heard the voices calling from the past, it tore through her, pulled at the basic building blocks of her genetic makeup, stirred the essence of her DNA, so that she rebounded with all of her being, and was made wild, ethereal, weightless, and then senseless with the animal motion.

The lights flickered and pulsed, and her eyes narrowed into slits, then opened wide with dilated pupils, while sweat issued from primeval pores and seeped down her pale gold skin. She bounced and sprang, threw her head back and forward, self-hypnotizing, pounding the floor with her feet, wanting to break past it into the earth itself, throwing her arms out to embrace the air and to rake with her nails the drafts that slithered over her surface.

When she was all white fire, her lungs scalded and gasping at the thin oxygen, needing a richer ancient draught, she collapsed, her feet stopping, while she stood panting and doubled over.

"Stop music . . ." she managed to whisper, and the harmonium obliged.

Ancient reeds faded, slipped into non-being, and the strings vibrato dissipated into silence. The last percussion beat clashed and fell, and was no more.

And Liaei stood panting, in the silent and now dark room, while tears streamed down her face and she sobbed convulsively from the gut, for what was gone, for the voices of her ancestors wrenched out of time, remembering she was so alone and they who were most like her were all no longer.

"The human sexual act resulted in a great deal of pleasure for the male and female," said the harmonium. "Not all other species experienced the same during mating, and often there was pain involved in the moments during the release of hormones. But for homo sapiens, mating and pleasure became a social obsession, and coupling and monogamy was more than the means of continuing the race but formed the economy and family structure. Casual and serious relationships evolved into various phases in a range between monogamy and polyamory, based on current economic and social conditions, and often discounting the needs and wants of the individuals—not to mention the needs of various same-gender and transitional-gender combinations of the so-called homosexual and otherwise differentiated portion of the population. But in the long run what drove it all was the physical need of the male and the female, and then simply the hormonal need of any individual for another individual, regardless of sexual orientation, and based only upon the emotional need for love."

"Yes, love . . ." mused Liaei, listening to the machine's lecture. "What a silly thing the ancients made of it by associating it with sex. What does love—genuine bonds of affection—have to do with hormonal excitement? Sorry, I don't get it. I mean, I do, on a strange remote level, but I also understand how illusory that connection is."

"You have reached the hormonal balance such as that you can understand sexual desire now, Liaei?" asked the harmonium.

There was no lurid shadow in that question, and yet something made Liaei blush as she heard it. And in that same moment as she felt herself grow warm with the strange embarrassment, she self-reflexively understood what she was doing and how odd it was to feel shame.

"It must be vulnerability . . ." she muttered to herself. "The shame and the blushing is related to vulnerability, an opening to intimacy. The surrendering of self, the loss of power, must result in initial fear." And for some reason she thought of the tech Toliwe, and the warmth on the surface of her skin intensified.

The harmonium continued. It described in detail the physical structures of the female and male bodies that were involved in the reproductive moment. "In the earlier young homo sapiens species, the male procreative organ, the penis was much larger, and more responsive to stimuli. The engorging with blood resulted in a stiffening and expansion of its tissues which the modern human genitals no longer experience. The female genitals were also deeper and more sensitive to hormonal fluctuation and to engorgement that paralleled the male organ on a smaller scale, in the small organ called the clitoris. The ancient vagina had to be able to expand enough to receive the swollen male organs and later to allow the newborn child to pass from the body—that flexibility was also a function of hormone levels and blood circulation. The modern female has a rudimentary vaginal canal that cannot accept any entry, and the womb and ovaries are pseudo-organs. The clitoris has devolved to such a tiny size that in most women it cannot be located. The modern male penis is a tiny blunt urinary ovoid protuberance of passive soft tissue, and the vestige testes have receded near the perineum. None are sensitive to ero-tactile stimulation."

"I am such a freak . . ." muttered Liaei. She thought of her own body with its deep vaginal canal and viable womb and functional ovaries and. . . .

"Not at all," replied the machine. "You are perfectly normal for your genetic makeup."

"And I am so sick of hearing that," she said, getting up, and then slammed the surface of the desk with her fist.

"Please don't hurt yourself. To change the subject, let us switch to the duties that await the Queen of the Hourglass," said the machine without missing a beat. "The seduction ritual is an important part of what will happen when you are with the Clock King, and the importance of the background material will become clear. Much of what we have discussed as foreplay is necessary for the sexual levels of arousal that initiate the reproductive process."

"You know what? I really don't want to hear it. So just shut yourself up," said Liaei tiredly. Then added, "Sorry, I mean, let's just continue this tomorrow, okay? I feel like crap."

Liaei hated to admit this to anyone, and especially to the medicineal techs who now measured every aspect of her development, but she was restless. Hormones were awash in her body, and her energy was boundless, so that she thought she could jump up and soar. On the other hand she did not mind admitting this to the harmonium.

"Feeling better today, Liaei?" it asked her, as she arrived for the next morning's lesson.

"Yes. Sorry about yesterday," said Liaei, yawning, and holding her hands around a warm mug of tonic herbal brew that she brought with her from the cafeteria.

The daylight was barely beginning to color the sky, and the patch of it in the overhead skylight was soft and dilute mauve.

"Today's lesson is seduction," said the harmonium. "It involves a buildup of excitement so that copulation becomes imminent, and is achieved by a combination of human skin contact, visual enticement, auditory stimulation, subtle smell, and a number of other environmental factors. Little of this can be described, and most must be experienced in practice. Regretfully I cannot show you much beyond the ancient so-called porn, short slang for pornography, which is visual recordings of homo sapiens copulating, for the sole purpose of eliciting sexual arousal or lust in the audience. Pornography was a powerful quasi-legal factor in the societies of all the civilizations of which we have records. Glimpses of it could be observed in the arts, music, even fashion of clothing and architecture. For thousands of years, sex and its mystique shaped the entertainment industries, drove the development of technology, and the staying power of it was such that even now, after the sex drive has dissipated in the species, some modern humans still attempt to capitalize on it, to recapture the energy and the allure, the animal life force—"

"Yeah, I know," said Liaei. "Some people in the clubs talk about gettogethers to watch the old fuckfests. They laugh, of course. It means nothing to them, just an ancient nature documentary. But I am afraid. They invited me once, and I really wanted to go and—and *see*. But I was afraid that it would have a different effect on me. I did not want to turn into a savage in front of them, to lose control."

"The possibility is very low that you would lose control under such circumstances, Liaei. According to our records, there is a difference between sex-based entertainment and the actual act."

Liaei shivered. "Okay, good to know. Do you think you can show me the porn, then?"

"Of course," replied the harmonium. "Let's start with the more softcore also known as erotica, and then we can build you up to the hardcore variants. Please feel free to stop the displays at any time and ask questions. In fact, you are encouraged to ask, since much of it can seem to make little sense, and is based on various individual fetishes throughout history."

"So, you managed to see some of that antique porn?" said Amhama chuckling and shaking her head as they were eating dinner. "Does any of it make sense to you, girl? I mean, at least your hormonal levels may make it more interesting for you.

Just to think, they used to have obsessions over body parts and body size, used to have grotesque operations to modify organs such as the female breasts. At the same time, many of their societies had rigid moral rules and weird intolerance in regard to the true range of gender. Makes you wonder why so much dissonance."

Liaei blushed then laughed, and continued to chew the hot spicy soya protein and vegetables. "It's rather amazing actually. There were enormous genitalia, breasts and buttocks, long legs and smooth or hairy chests, contorted backs and various other limbs, and these red colored lips—all huge and exaggerated. Actually, no, not always huge—they were of all shapes and sizes. But always something was exaggerated in those displays, to the point of grotesque. At least the early super-archaic stuff was all live real human video or stills. But then this computer simulart took over. The animated porn just went all caricature, with almost insectoid body distortion, and unreal motion.

"Oh, and you wouldn't believe the things they were wearing! Clothing that served no other function but emphasis of certain body parts. Full or partial nudity, and one or more men or women involved, group scenes. And they had toys— implements? There was even some truly disgusting subject matter. I mean, I had no idea, but anything and everything— body fluids, inanimate objects, food, force, pain, other animal species, even auditory playacting—could serve as sexual turn- ons for the ancients. You know, Ama, I was afraid at first, afraid that I'd respond to any of this, but then it just got to be ridiculous. Too much maybe, for one sitting. I started to giggle and then laughed for hours, watching. Laughed and laughed. . . ."

Liaei suddenly put her utensils down with a clatter and raised her fingers to rub against her burning cheeks. "I am blushing again, damn it, aren't I?" she said. "Oh, why do I have to take it all so personally? It's as if I am embarrassed for all of them and their focused naturalism—primitivism, I should say—

as if I take responsibility for all the foibles of the ancient race. Why, why, damn it, why—"

Amhama watched her with a meaningful expression and even put her spoon to rest in the bowl. "It's all right, Liaei. Really, it is, keep telling yourself. Now, if it does affect you at some point, sweet, don't feel bad. For you it would be a normal thing to feel *something*. Always remember that. There's nothing wrong with that, nothing wrong with having a living response."

"Sure, Ama, whatever," said Liaei. And then she began to either laugh or cry, rubbing her face in her hands, and taking in convulsive gasps of air into her primitive lungs.

Amhama continued to watch, frozen with sympathy and impotence.

Liaei was obsessed with imagining Toliwe nude. It seemed absurd in her own mind, especially after the visual overload of the antique lurid images she had seen of naked male and female flesh in intimate contact. But her young curiosity was a driving force, as powerful and erratic in its fluctuations and intensity as her life energy. Toliwe was an ordinary man, and yes, she had seen the banal anatomy of modern male genitalia numerous times, and yes this was nothing new. And yet. . . .

At the gym, when she and Toliwe did the workouts every other day, Liaei would sneak glimpses of his androgynous body in motion.

The local gym was a large well-lit complex with a high ceiling of transparent glassoid to allow in the bright Day God light. In addition to the usual full-body tone machines, steppers, runwalks, rowers, weights, stretchers, muscle-stims, there was much aerial equipment for the latest modern exercise fad, Sky Dancing or SD. Music with a very light underlying on-off binary rhythm filled the place, and the overhead expanse was always occupied with at least three or four people at a time doing one or more of the suspended forms of Sky Dance, using the hand-swingers, the aero-spin, or the ever-popular wings.

Toliwe was great at Sky Dancing. They had come in today after dinner, their group of five consisting of Toliwe, Liaei, and three other horticulturist techs, Chwanta, Finnei and Olato.

Olato was the youngest of the techs, just fresh out of school, and his handsome earnest face was sweetened by an easy smile. He was pale gold, a faint and delicate hue, and his smooth skin overlay defined musculature. Olato worked out more than anyone else Liaei knew, and right now he and Toliwe had gone up to the aerials and were swinging by their arms, strong hands gripping the handlebars, on their way to the upper rung advanced SD equipment. Both were dressed in loose-clinging natural fiber sweat pants and t-shirts that rippled in the faint breeze of the overhead air vents.

Liaei and the two women were still on the floor equipment. Chwanta, taller and darker than everyone and lithe like a thing of molten metal—Liaei thought—was finishing the five kilometer run cycle on the runwalk, her limbs flashing deep bronze as she sped in place, arms and elbows pumping, knees contracting and expanding in rhythm, and legs flying. Chwanta's smooth head, beautifully oval, was thrown back and beads of sweat made tracks along the contours of her scalp, face, neck and chest, sinking into the absorbent fibers of her red sport shirt. Her eyes were closed and she was panting slightly in measured powerful intakes and exhales while the equipment voice-over recited the remaining distance.

"Almost done . . ." she gasped, without opening her eyes, "Hold on just a little, everyone, all right? Don't go up without me."

"Sure," said Liaei who had just finished her stretching routine on the mats followed by a series of balanced extended handstands against the support wall. She was adjusting the band that was holding up her mane of hair into a gathered tail and considered twisting and then tying it up into a bun contraption that she had seen an antique woman do in—of all places—one of the ancient live porn displays.

From the back, Finnei tugged gently at Liaei's tail of hair, saying in her sonorous voice, "Don't, just leave it swinging, Li. I like it that way."

Liaei turned to stare at Finnei with a slightly self-conscious expression. She always felt that way when her physical differences were in any way drawn attention to.

Finnei was one of the most beautiful young women that Liaei knew. Even now after the bit of teasing, as she watched Liaei with her eyes the color of the iridescent surface film of Oceanus water, Liaei could not ignore her other attributes. Her skin appeared pearly silver-rose; an exquisite bone structure underlay her scalp; her nose had a delicately sculpted bridge that gave way to a charming, slightly upturned tip with fine chiseled nostrils. Finnei's lips were somewhat fuller than average, curved and soft. She was very slim and her black sports top hugged a perfect flat chest with tiny buds of nipples, while underneath were toned hips and long powerfully muscled legs, clad in shorts. Two sensitized metal studs were embedded in the pierced lobes of Finnei's ears, metal contrasting with pearlescent skin, and the cabochon surfaces danced in a shimmering surface motion with the smallest change of light.

"What?" said Finnei, grinning at Liaei's sour expression. "I love your hair, Li, really. I wish I had some. Just think of all the curious things I could do with it, build braid geo-structures over my head, organize the individual hair follicles into fractal weaves of high intricacy . . ."

Liaei knew the other was being kind and meant well. But she could never escape the underlying subtle sense that they were all just fondly tolerating her, as though she were a weirdly sentient pet animal or plant—an exotic specimen of another primitive species who was entrusted under their watchful care. Even their pointed kindness grated at Liaei.

And Finnei's goodwill grated in particular. Liaei did not miss the profound looks that Finnei and Toliwe exchanged with one another when they thought the others were otherwise preoccupied.

Looks of intimacy, the kind that led to Life Bonding.

At the thought of it, a painful wrenching sensation came inside Liaei's chest, somewhat unlocalized, and caused by nerve spasms which in turn were caused by the thoughts.

Well, why not, Liaei thought, forcing herself to experience the alien pangs. Why not, when it would make perfect sense for Toliwe to bond with someone like Finnei, an older, subtle, wise woman. Serious in some ways, just like him.

They had so much in common, those two. Brilliant, intellectual.

"Done!" panted Chwanta as her runwalk came to an even halt. She jumped off, wiping her forehead and back of the neck, and said, "Give me a moment and then let's go up."

Overhead, Toliwe already soared, locked in the wings, his powerful arm and thigh muscles rhythmically pumping the kinetic energy via connecting pulleys into the generators attached at the wing bases to harmonium converters. The harmonium in turn used the kinetic energy to power the movement of the wings which spun like sharp deadly blades and kept the user aloft, treading air. It was the ultimate culmination of the Sky Dance exercise routine.

Once he hit the rhythm, Toliwe could tread air for hours.

Next to Liaei, Finnei looked up, momentarily watching Toliwe with a smile, then waved at Olato who had engaged the aero-spin and was whirling so fast that his golden shape was a blur.

"He can't see you, silly," said Chwanta, holding a water-conserving gym towel to her face, still cooling off.

"Ah, but he can," said Finnei with a mischievous smile that crinkled the skin at the bridge of her delicate nose. "Toliwe says there's an amazing point of balance during the aero-spin when you can actually learn to spot and focus on a specific landmark, so that there is this weird stereophonic visual awareness of all the points around you, relative to that mark."

"I don't think Olato's that advanced yet," said Chwanta with a chuckle.

Liaei remained quiet. Indeed she was always somewhat uncomfortable with heights, and aero-spin made her dizzy and even sick, something to do with the balance in her inner ear, she was told. She preferred to stick to the beginner hand-swingers and just watch the others do the more advanced stuff.

And that way she could look at Toliwe, watch him move.

"I am going up," said Finnei. And then she glanced at Liaei. "Coming, Li?"

Liaei nodded, and then the three of them began to ascend the stair-bars to the SD equipment section.

Reaching the top, Finnei released the final staircase cross-bar and stood up on the platform. She then spread out her hands and took an elegant dive forward through the air and caught the first hand swinger with a sure grip of both hands.

With a gentle hum the exercise machine came alive and started to rotate along its drum axis, so that new handlebars came into view along its edges with the slow initial rotation. Finnei gripped each handlebar with alternating right then left hands and with her motion and distribution of weight the rotation of the hand swinger drum increased until Finnei hung upright rapidly moving her hands in place to keep up.

Eventually the hand swinger moved forward, its cycle near the middle, while a second hand swinger emerged from the overhead compartment, descended in place for the next user.

Liaei's turn was next.

Her heart beginning to pound in silent terror of the abyss of empty space before her, Liaei forced herself to move forward. There was the remote awareness of the safety nets stretched taut below the aerial portion of the gym, but it was not enough for the irrational ancient part of her. She emptied her mind with a force of will, inhaled deeply and at the same time plunged toward the bars hovering in the air less than a meter before her. For one sickening second she felt the imminent weightless void—the safety nets seemed a thousand meters away below— and then her hands connected with the bars and she landed with a jarring initial shock, holding on in an instinctive death grip. As the instrument began to move, she forced herself again to unclench her grip, and never looking down, grabbed for the first new bar on her right, then the second one on the left, and so on.

Only several meters ahead of her Finnei was effortlessly nearing the end of the cycle and saying something to Olato who had stopped aero-spinning and then to Toliwe who was doing yet another cycle on the wings. There was casual laughter.

They never knew what terror clamored inside Liaei. She made sure each time that they would not know, especially that Toliwe never would.

"The difference between modern Life Bonding and the similar ancient social rituals," said the harmonium, "those inter-personal affirmation rituals of the extinct people whose genetic material was closest to yours—was mostly economics. At first, contracts between individuals were superseded by contracts between families, tribes, even nations. And for the earliest homo sapiens the contract was valid only between a man and a woman pair. It was only after several thousand years had passed that same-sex bonding was legally recognized. And by then the economic rules had relaxed enough that pair and group bonding became the choice of the individuals involved only, regardless of gender, but still based on sex drive and, when applicable, medical conditions."

Liaei sipped from her mug of morning tea. "So then, this sex-based form of social slavery was abolished and people were free to desire and bond as they wanted?"

"Essentially, yes," the harmonium responded. "Since economics were no longer based on groups but on individuals. Each individual of the species became a unique resource. As a result, the power of decision belonged to that individual alone. Much of this was concurrent with the evolution of individual rights. Rights guaranteed personal freedoms, and set specific societal safeguarding limits, and in the long run it guaranteed sovereignty of the human unit."

"I cannot imagine inter-human slavery of any sort," Liaei said, as the morning light came to fall on her face from overhead through the skylight, painting her skin warm mist-gold, and rendering her hair into metallic fire. "Even now, it is bad enough we are slaves to our own personalities, to duty, to what we believe is right, to resources. But to be enslaved by the idiotic and arbitrary selfish will of another, even if they are a family member? Must have been infuriating, frustrating, impossible. No wonder those poor abused people died so young after such tormented lives."

"Modern Life Bonding is based on affection and personal compatibility," the harmonium said. "But it was not so before the sex drive became extinct. The power of hormonal urges was so strong in the ancients that sexual attraction was the primary factor for bonding, and then came all other reasons, even though this was publicly denied by all involved. The union of commitment called marriage, in its brief historical period when it was based on love, resulted in separations, divorces and frequent cheating on the contract, called adultery. The one positive of this supremely brief period was that the cheaters at least were not punished as severely as they had been in the even earlier times when the marriage contract was not based on the love-sex complex but economics. In those dark ages of humanity the contract breakers were often punished by severe social shunning, corporal punishment, mutilation, and even death."

"What?" said Liaei with a snort. "Death for no longer wanting to be with someone? Oh, Day God. . . ."

At that point someone had come up from behind and touched Liaei on the shoulder. The contact was gentle, but she started, since she was already trembling from what the harmonium had just said.

It was Amhama.

"Ama? What are you doing here? I am still in class," said Liaei.

Amhama's normally placid soft face was more tense than normal. "Sorry to interrupt," she said. "But Riveli needs to see you now."

"Why? What about? I am not scheduled with her until the day after tomorrow."

"I know. But this is something that just came up. Riveli will see both of us."

Riveli's office visit was as clinically dull as usual, except for the somewhat unexpected announcement that Liaei will be assuming her role as the Queen of the Hourglass next year as opposed to the two years she had been told recently.

"Have you had sexual urges, Liaei?" Riveli asked suddenly, after she had asked all the usual questions. "Do you find yourself regularly thinking about physical stimulation? Have you experienced sexually stimulating dreams, or attempted to stimulate yourself in any way?"

The room seemed very chill all of a sudden.

Liaei became motionless.

But Riveli did not seem to notice as she continued, "And do you think more than usual, and more intimately than usual, about any persons you know? For example, any male persons, male techs? Intimate thoughts are natural at this point—"

Liaei, sitting on the edge of the beige fabric-upholstered chair, stared at Riveli in thunderstruck silence, while Amhama clenched her hands in the corner seat.

Riveli shook her head then sighed. "Come now, no need to be shy or embarrassed, my dear, I am your medcare giver. This is all normal for someone in your situation, with your hormonal makeup and genetics."

"If that's the case," Liaei said with an empty face, and in a strange calm voice, "then why ask me these personal prying questions? You say I am normal, so there's the answer. You know all about me from the regular tech diagnostic reports. You have samples of all my tissues and bodily fluids. Would you like me to void myself now and bring you the most recent—"

"Liaei!" said Amhama. "Please don't be rude. . . ."

"All right. I won't. I am sorry, Riveli."

Her voice was like ice. Liaei got up and without saying another word walked out of the office.

News of her rebellion spread. The horticulturist techs who worked with Liaei that week acted and talked to her with such care that Liaei was even more infuriated and embarrassed. In the medicineal cafeteria stares followed her more than usual as she walked between the food selection aisles and seated eaters. When she got home each night, Amhama said nothing but looked at her with what Liaei thought was pity.

Liaei ate her dinner, then cleaned up after the two of them, then immediately went to her room and locked the door after herself. She knew Amhama would sit at her harmonium display in the living room, pretending to be reading despite the sounds of savage ancient music that clearly seeped through the inadequate insulation of the door.

Let her think I am sexually stimulating myself like a primitive in the porn displays, thought, Liaei, standing before her mirror and watching the flow of her hair, loosened and long against her shoulders, the hairs overlying in twin arches her browline, the lashes surrounding her eyes. With her hands she brushed the surface of her arms with its fine almost invisible hair . . . everywhere.

The music thundered around her, and the lights flickered to the savage percussion beat, while a man and woman dead for a million years sang in discord and harmony, wailing out of the past and pulling at the lump in her throat. She tried to imagine them jumping around, torsos twisting, hips gyrating, contorting, naked, twined around one another with virile limbs soaking in wanton perspiration that did not have to be recycled, massage oil and pheromones, while their hair-covered skin mingled and fused in the act of mindless burning desire.

Her personal razor tool, specially made to accommodate the trimming of her long head hair, was in its place in her grooming cabinet. Liaei picked it up, unfolded the safety lock to reveal the short field of micro-blades and looked at it. Then, standing in front of the mirror again, she lifted the foremost lock of hair over her forehead in a taut grip and sheared it off, directly against the skin, leaving a bare spot. The skin which the hair had covered was pristine and paler than the rest of her face.

As she worked, she hummed along with the music in a low sonorous voice.

"Liaei! Oh, what have you done to yourself?" Chwanta exclaimed when Liaei came in for her first daily test.

Liaei's head formerly covered by a luxurious mane of hair was now a bare smooth scalp with the faintest hint of subdermal stubble. Instead of eyebrows, she had pale shadow-lines over her brow areas. Her eyes were red-rimmed because she had pulled out all her eyelashes and the skin was inflamed. And her arms and legs, what was visible from underneath her clothing were bare of hair also.

Liaei shrugged.

Chwanta, who today was wearing a sterile coat and held a harmonium pad, put the pad away on her cluttered desk, and approached Liaei.

It was only then that Liaei was stricken by the comprehension of what she had done. Chwanta's normally placid expression was replaced by an intense stare and a focus of such concern that Liaei was afraid.

"Why did you do it?" said Chwanta. She put both her hands on Liaei's shoulders, and just stood waiting.

But Liaei had no overt explanation. To say "I want to look like everyone else" was too trite. She was already pathetic in so many ways that such a blatant call for attention was more humiliating than anything she could imagine.

Liaei smiled, and maybe it was unnatural, but Chwanta did not know her well enough in that sense to judge. Chwanta knew all about her heart rate and estrogen balance and fluid circulation. Chwanta knew that Liaei liked to eat spicy foods and did not fancy heights. But not how she smiled when she was trying to lie.

"Don't worry," said Liaei gently, as though she was the one to be consoled. "It will grow back soon enough. I am trying to see what it's like to look like all the rest of you, for a change. Yeah, I know it's a silly fashion phase, but just humor me for now."

"Oh, Li," said Chwanta. "You are beautiful and your natural growth of hair is lovely, and you are fine just exactly the way you were formed—perfect, in fact. If anything is bothering you, if you want to talk about anything at all, you know you can talk to me, all right?"

"Sure."

Chwanta exhaled in relief. "All right, then, and you look cute, girl!" She drew her tickling fingers over Liaei's bare scalp.

"Thanks."

The rest of the daily test went on as usual. Chwanta took organ function measurements and when all was done, waved at Liaei, saying she'll see her later tonight. "Have fun with the harmonium's history of gender differences lecture."

Liaei nodded with the same soft smile, and then headed to see Toliwe. Harmonium time came later; for now she had other plans.

Toliwe was in the development lab on the 78th floor of the medicineal, where he normally checked Liaei's breathing patterns and lung capacity. Liaei walked into the room noiselessly, more self-conscious than usual. She did not look at ecosystems of transparent glassoid which lined the walls, and where various living plant and animal cells grew in gaseous fluid cocktails of mauve and amber and green hues under a variety of illumination.

She looked at the man who stood with his back to her, focused intently on his task of processing genetic material through micro-filtering equipment.

Toliwe had on the requisite sterile coat, and held a bouquet of fine transparent tubes in one hand, delicately playing each tube with an agile finger when needed, which extended to various living mass containers on the work surface. With the other hand he directed a beam of harmonium-tuned energy from a fine pointing device which activated and shaped the arrangement of genetic material inside living cells.

Liaei watched his silhouette, the smooth head, strong but slender neck, coat fabric covering wide tapering shoulders.

A spasm of nerves squeezed her throat, but she forced herself to speak.

"Hi . . . I'm early."

Toliwe's shape froze for a moment, then without turning around he continued the complex set of motions with his hands, saying, "I'll be with you in a moment. Go on and sit down."

Liaei obeyed, and walked over to the other side of the lab where the lung machine was, and sat down in one of the chairs. With movement she felt the air wash over her naked scalp, and it was an odd feeling. She was still not used to it, the cold and vulnerability.

As she sat waiting for him, her arms itched. She'd removed hair from every possible surface of her body. Her eyelids itched also, but she knew not to touch them so as not to induce an infection. Idle moments poured in an endless stream.

Toliwe finally came around, tired and reserved as always, carrying his usual data pad. Only this time, seeing Liaei he stopped. His handsome face did not show any significant change of expression, but Liaei knew, because she had watched him so closely for so long, that when he stilled like that it meant he was paying attention.

"What happened to your hair?" Toliwe asked.

Liaei laughed and shrugged. "I got tired of it. Wanted to try another look. What do you think?"

"Oh," he said.

"So, what do you think?"

"Fine either way. I like it, but I think your head of hair looked just as good. It was natural to you."

"Oh." This time she said it.

Toliwe was staring at her, it seemed. Or maybe not. Maybe he was looking blankly, as he usually did.

Liaei felt cold gripping her, nervous clenching, spasms in her gut.

"Go ahead and grab the breathing tube," Toliwe said after another brief moment, and turned to engage the lung machine. It was going to be the extent of his reaction, Liaei realized.

As the harmonium energy field came alive with a hum that was just out of human hearing range, but giving off vibrations that were still tactile, Liaei held the long pale tube end and breathed into it rhythmically, the best she could. She was feeling short of breath and somewhat lightheaded.

The data drum began to turn and Toliwe observed the incoming data dots, then frowned slightly. "Your exhalations are weaker than normal today," he said. "Are you feeling okay?"

His cool voice struck Liaei with a jarring impact, and more spasms echoed in her gut and chest.

She forced herself with a superhuman effort to relax, and started taking deeper breaths, so as to produce richer exhalations.

Toliwe glanced at her a couple of times with his beautiful dark eyes. For the rest of the test he said nothing.

"As the Queen of the Hourglass, you will need to master the art of sensual movement, which is one of the key elements of seduction," said the harmonium.

Liaei sat half-listening, one hand propping up her cheek, and the tips of her fingers brushing absentmindedly against the faint stubble at the edge of her scalp. All of her body surfaces from which she had removed hair itched, and now she wished she had not removed her animalistic coating. Only a day had passed and already it was growing back. And her new habit was to feel the stubble, to run her fingers against the growth on her head, arms, and legs.

"Since you like to dance, Liaei," the harmonium said, "you will probably enjoy this portion of your sexuality education."

The display screen came alive.

"Unfortunately we have no other records of real ancient sex dance, except for this one synthetic digitalization of something called belly dance. And it is also regrettable that the image used in the animation is not of a homo sapiens female but an artificially generated composite creature with some of the sexually prized proportions of the female human body but the head and hindquarters of an extinct mammalian animal called a cat. Try to imagine the rest of the body as human as you observe the very brief display."

"Oh, great," said Liaei.

A rhythmic percussion and wailing wind instrument soundtrack came on, and the display crackled in broken-up frames of the million-year-old recording. Bluish-green background took on rudimentary perspective as a female cartoon creature with greatly exaggerated spherical breasts, pronounced recessed umbilical cord area, and round hips began to undulate. The feline head of the image had long eyelashes that it batted over great unnatural round eyes, and it swished its tail in curving arcs as it moved. Back and forth the hips ground, covered with a thin low-slung belt of shining material and tassels, while the strange giant mammaries jiggled under their presumed weight. The creature waved its plump arms in delicate soft curves, and clicked some kind of tiny snapping instrument with the fingertips. As the performance ground to a halt, the cat woman pouted with her swollen human female lips that grew in size, nearly filling up the display area, and were colored the typical red. She made a kiss sound, then flicked a pink tongue provocatively.

The display faded.

Liaei snorted. "You really expect me to do something like that belly dance?"

"Try it when you get home," the harmonium said.

"Liaei, girl, aren't you going to have something to eat? I made us a spicy amaranth and corn medley, with leeks and freshly ground pepper, homelab made. I cultivated the pepper DNA myself just last week, and it worked out wonderfully, cayenne—"

Amhama's voice came from the other side of the locked door to Liaei's room. Liaei had locked it from the inside, and now stood before the tall mirror. She replied, "I'm not hungry yet, thanks! A little later, Ama!"

"All right, but don't wait too long because it tastes better freshly warm, not reheated. The full strength of the pungent spice has been released and the leftovers will be of weaker potency—"

The window to her bedroom was open, and the Day God-gilded Basin walls were shining bright, and reflecting upon the narrow visible strip of Oceanus. Arid wind moved the pale fabric curtains, and the light and movement reflected in the mirror, in which Liaei's backlit form was a dark silhouette.

"Music, 3/4 measure, balanced percussion beat, rate very slow to medium fast to slow fadeout, wind and strings, no voices."

Sound filled the room, swelling out of the air itself, it seemed.

Liaei watched her own silhouette moving with grace to the beginning notes. She removed her clothes, swaying with the sound, gently, trying to keep her body fluid and confident. When she was completely nude, she looked at her own dark silhouette and its natural curves. Without the usual curtain of hair over her head, for the first time she saw the true balance of her body. The proportions were mathematically pleasing, with shoulders and hips being almost parallel, and the narrow inward-curving line of waist was cinched parallel to her slender line of neck. Narrow and wide, in aesthetic balance. Her legs, when drawn together, tapered into equally narrow feet, which echoed the neck and head dimensions.

Liaei squinted her eyes, relaxing her imagination, and a visual gestalt formed, of two masses, vaguely triangular or even circular, one on top of the other. It was the prehistoric mathematical symbol of infinity flipped on its side.

And if she squinted and blinked, it approximated the same general proportions of the ancient device called the hourglass.

Toliwe seemed more remote than usual to Liaei. If it were possible, he was avoiding her, and yet she knew it was not the case, not with someone like Toliwe. He was forthright and stubborn and wise, and he never shirked facing his duty and responsibility—such as herself.

At their regular checkup appointments, Toliwe was reserved and polite, when needed, gentle, and he seemed capable of facing her calmly. And yet there was something very subtle, a new barrier between them. Sometimes it was a mere difference of seconds—moments fewer spent in her company than possible.

Yes, they would still meet at the gym, sometimes with a group of other techs, sometimes just the two of them, but Liaei noticed now that Toliwe had learned to be impeccable in never crossing the line between a professional relationship and friendship.

Liaei's hair was coming back. She now had a soft fuzzy centimeter-high buzz growth on her head, pale flax. Her lashes and brows too were regrowing, coming in a bit bristly and not as soft as they had originally been.

"You're like a brush, you realize?" Amhama said often, patting her on the hair. "I still don't understand why you cut it off in the first place, but I suppose it is a good thing you did it once, so now you know how it is."

"No problem," said Liaei in a flippant banter. "My next thing is to get my earlobes pierced, like Finnei."

Amhama smiled, shaking her head.

Thus Liaei had learned to placate Amhama with the semblance of youthful rebellion. It was easier to act out than what was really inside.

It was early spring of the year of the Day God 51,003 Post Harmonium, about 4 months after Liaei had cut off her hair for no clear reason, that the psychological truce between Liaei and Toliwe reached a crisis.

They were walking along the crystallized and calcified shoreline of the Oceanus, salt encrusted between the water and the land like pale exquisite lace. All around the Basin walls towered, filling the vista, and directly in zenith stood the golden swollen light of the Day God, poured into all of sky. The Oceanus wind reeked of toxic matter as it wafted inland.

Toliwe was several steps ahead of her, and Liaei walked with her gaze down, watching the sharp rocks and the occasional partially buried remains of old water pipes under her sport shoes—rocks and boulders striated orange, rose, cream. The wind was warm, and it swept them in irregular gusts, taking Liaei's breath away momentarily. On one of the slopes a jagged, razor-thin meandering line of white fire marked The River That Flows Through The Air.

The pier that was the spot of their usual exercise was only a few meters away.

It was at that point that Toliwe, glancing sideways to his right, and somewhat stiffer than usual in his movements, suddenly tripped and lost his footing. He didn't make a sound, only slid down the gravel incline, stopping only several steps away from the thick inky water, right in the middle of the pale crystalline salt growth on the edges that separated the water from the land.

"Toliwe!" exclaimed Liaei. She scrambled after him down the slope.

Toliwe was already up on his feet, hands covered with pale salt, and was shaking off the seat of his jeans, and limping. His bronze scalp glistened with sudden moisture. When he turned his face toward her, Liaei saw him wince with pain.

"Damn . . ." he said. "Liaei, I am sorry, looks like I am not going to be able to do the stretching balance routine with you today."

"Are you okay?" she said, knowing he was not okay but needing to say it out loud. She leaned toward him and then crouched to observe his right foot, already swollen at the ankle and the torn leg of his jeans.

"I don't think anything's broken," he replied. "Probably just a bad sprain. Hurts to step on it, so you'll need to help me walk up the slope."

"Of course . . ." She locked his right arm with hers, stiff in all of her body at the contact, and afraid to press, afraid to feel what she was holding, and yet his arm was firm and warm. They walked slowly with measured steps up the incline, while small rocks came clattering from under their feet. Once on the pier, Liaei helped him sit down on the warmed ground, with his right foot stretched out in front of him, elevated slightly.

She stood away, releasing his arm, releasing the strange warm solid bond, and just stood there, watching him as he pressed the voice comm on his datapad and requested medical assistance from the medicineal. He spoke in a controlled level voice, not giving any indication of his true discomfort, and only his facial expression seemed more grim than usual, facial muscles nearly frozen, the black pupils of his eyes dilated in pain.

When he was done, Toliwe looked up at her and made the effort of a grin. "They'll be here soon," he said. "Meanwhile, why don't you go ahead and do the routine as usual? Pretend I am doing it too. Here, let me first set the recorder to take your heart rate measurements—"

Liaei stared at him, watching him struggle to seem normal. "Oh, come on," she said, frowning. "I can't do it now, now seeing you hurt!"

He winced again, his eyes narrowing, and then lifted a hand to shield his vision from the blazing orange light from overhead.

"Why not?" he said. "We are kind of stuck here, wasting time, and you might as well use it to your advantage."

Liaei felt her head spin with a sudden wildness. She crouched again, just centimeters away from him, so that they were seeing eye to eye and he did not have to make the extra effort to look up into the brightness of the Day God. For several long moments they stared.

Toliwe's expression was unreadable, but if she could smell fear, she was smelling it now.

"Do you know," she said, "that it would be a little crazy of me to be doing Fua motions with you like this? Do you really think I am such a quaint specimen of old DNA, so different from you, that even though we cannot technically mate you can discount me as a person? Liaei, jump, breathe, walk, dance! Liaei, do the Fua routine like a good little primitive bitch!"

"What do you mean . . ."

But she continued, coming down on her knees in front of him, then slumping and sitting down with her legs folded. "Don't you think of me in any other way than something weird that you grew in your lab?"

The stench of his fear was rising in her mind. She was not sure if it was his or her own, but she could not stop.

"Liaei," he tried, "I never imagined this—"

"That's because you only imagined the datapad readout, excellent progress, eh, Toliwe? I am doing so well, and you are so proud of me!"

"Of course I am proud of you!" For the first time his voice lost its calm and he made a movement with his body toward her, forgetting his injury, then winced in pain. His eyes had an expression of shock.

Liaei sat before him, her palms gripping the warm ground, while tears started blinding her, started to run in torrents down her face, and the wind swept dust into her eyes.

"You are proud of Liaei, the survivor, the viable Queen of the Hourglass, who will be fertile when the time comes and who will bear a child and enrich the gene pool, and—"

"Oh, no, Liaei!" he was speaking fast now, his hands—strong and firm and warm—pressing down her shoulders, pressing hard. "Listen to me, you are really upset because I think there's a misunderstanding between us, right? Liaei? What is it that you think that I think about you—or not think—I mean, I am not making any sense. You have strong feelings, you are young and intense and your hormonal levels are—"

"Oh yes, that's right!" she interrupted. "I knew you were going to mention hormones at one point or another! Well guess what? I am not just the sum of interacting chemicals and genetic soup, but a sentient being! And yes, I *feel!* There's joy and sorrow, and there's this other—this utter crap. Unlike you who are like this rock on which you are sitting, so stable, so intellectually and physically advanced, so wise and confident and beyond me. Hell, you have a million or so years of evolution on me!"

He was shaking his head, frown lines and pain lines mixed up in his face. "Oh Liaei, I am so sorry—"

She was floating away from him, cold and remote, looking through a curtain of tears. "Are we so different?" she said as she sobbed. "Are we like two different species? Show me your body, please, Toliwe, please . . . Let me see what you are, a man? I am a woman, and you are a man, how can we be so different and remote? How can you not feel? Why aren't you drawn to me, not even with the tiniest bit of something, some stupid chemical in your bloodstream—"

Speaking thus, she reached out with her hands, putting them to his chest, then drew the shaking palm of her right hand to stroke him, feeling the curve of body, the warmth.

But he took her hand in his, firmly and gently, and she realized that the fear she was smelling in him was pity.

Toliwe was looking at her, his eyes like dark jewels, moist, she realized, also like her own, his beautiful face tragic.

"You do know that what you are asking and insisting is a form of interpersonal harassment, Liaei? It would be a form of pressure, illegal and wrong, to force yourself on another individual, and if you were anyone else, it would be so. But—"

He paused, and then his grip tightened around her fingers, and then just as suddenly he was gentle, and he put his hands on the clasp of his jeans.

Liaei stared, terrified, as Toliwe undid the front of his clothing, then undid the pale layer of underclothing, exposing himself to her. She looked and saw what she knew to find there. A small blunt protuberance of flesh, skin almost colorless, washed out by the strong daylight, the organ flaccid and rudimentary. Not a trace of pubic hair. Not a trace of movement or life.

"Is this what you wanted to see?" he whispered, then slowly covered himself up again, and closed up the opening in his jeans. "I am sorry with all my heart, with all my ability to feel as a human being. I cannot feel what you want me to feel, for you or anyone. No means to respond, no way to give you what you want, what you have every right to have. I belong to a dying race, Liaei. The physical excitement is so faint, that it's like an echo. Yes, I feel something. But not enough to even name it. A shadow of desire."

"A shadow of desire . . ." she echoed him, and laughed and wept at the same time, using the back of her hand to wipe the running mess of her face.

And then he took her by the shoulders and drew her close, and he ran his hand through her short pale gold hair, that was now just covering her ears.

"I can feel intellectual affection, I can fall in love, but it is a thing of the mind," he whispered near her ear. "It is like a complex mathematical construct, wherein the physical contact of flesh is a tiny single-digit variable, and all the rest—affinity, thoughts, life experience, personality gestalt, even gestures and motion and appearance and tone of voice—all of it matter to create the desire to Bond. It is a desire of experience, not of a physical sensation. Does that make sense? A desire for shared time."

"Shared time . . . Common time, yes. I should understand this, being the Queen of the Hourglass, should I not?" she whispered suddenly, pausing in comprehension. Her voice was thick with misery, tears. It cracked, and then she coughed, sputtering against Toliwe's plain fiber shirt.

"Soon . . ." he said in his softest and most gentle tone. It was cryptic, yet not quite.

"You mean, soon the Clock King will be the one for me, to make the savage Bond and share Common Time with?" said Liaei. "While you and Finnei make your serene Bond with only a shadow of desire . . ."

"In a way . . ." he replied, watching her with kindness, and she was not sure whether he answered her first or second question.

It did not particularly matter. At that point an ambulance car approached, hovering a couple of meters over the crumbling sand and salt dust of the pier and leaving a smooth swept trail, and Liaei sat back, to give Toliwe space, and to allow the techs to assist him.

But the tension wall between them was now broken, and in the breaching of it, Liaei found a peculiar combination of newfound distance and proximity. The distance would be eternal, a dividing line of lack of common will. While the proximity was also permanent now, an understanding of sorts.

It was an understanding across genetic time.

Liaei menstruated for the first time just a month before her fifteenth birthday. She had been trained in what to expect and still it was traumatic. She woke up and used the voidroom, and there was blood.

"Ama!" she cried, holding the voidroom door partway closed for privacy, and looking out into the corridor through a narrow crack. "It's happened, Ama! Red discharge! What do I do? Where are the pads? Oh, Ama!"

Amhama felt a moment of panic herself. Putting her night robe on, she hurried to the hallway and rummaged through their closet for the specially made soaking pads, formulated just for Liaei's needs. Holding a couple, Amhama thrust them around the door and through the opening. Liaei's hand snaked forward, grabbing them.

"Are you sure it's blood?" said Amhama. "And are you sure it's coming from your vaginal area and not from an injury somewhere else? It's okay, sweet, just trying to be very certain here. It is wonderful if it's so! Congratulations! Oh, what a wonder this is!"

Fumbling and rustling sounds came from the other side of the door. Then, "Yes, I am sure . . . what else would it be? Red fruit juice?"

On the other side of the door Amhama laughed, trembling, rubbing one thin arm with the other, in a peculiar gesture of self-consolation. There was joy and amazement and fulfillment of many years of work and not daring to hope, and then expectation. Amhama felt as proud as if she had been the girl's mother in the ancient genetic and gestational sense.

But, standing in the half-light of the hallway, thin and pale gold, Amhama looked just as she did fourteen years ago. Those times of intimate motherhood were long past. Such physical experience was alien to Amhama. Her glacial rate of aging was a reminder of the difference between her and her heart's child who will live and die in such an ephemeral span.

Now, it was almost time to let go.

"I've made arrangements, and you will be assuming your role of the Queen of the Hourglass next week," said Riveli in a far more gentle tone than she'd used for years.

Liaei and Amhama were seated in stiff silence in the chief nurse's office.

"How do you feel, Liaei?" Riveli continued. She was seated at her desk and as always observing her harmonium display as she talked. Liaei wondered if this was merely a safety barrier in her communication style or whether Riveli was indeed so infernally busy that she could never take a moment away from her minutiae of work and make consistent eye contact like a normal person.

"Fine," Liaei said.

"Good. Do you feel you are ready?"

Liaei's eyes focused somewhere just ahead of her, staring at a spot on the wall, while her lips moved into a smile. She took a deep breath, exhaled loudly, then said, "Yes."

"Excellent. I've contacted the Committee up at Edge City, and we think it is the right time to proceed with the project. My colleague up there, horticulturist medic Vioma, will take over my supervisory duties and you will be well cared in her charge. Once you get there, they will train you briefly in the Protocol and then you will become the Queen of the Hourglass."

For the first time Amhama spoke up. "How will Liaei travel to Edge City?"

Riveli stood up and faced them.

"You know about the risks of inter-city travel. It's a sterile wasteland out there, filled with bio-hazard. We cannot exactly risk putting her in an air transport, not all the way up the Basin slope."

Amhama frowned. "Why not?" she said. "What's wrong with the air transports? I know we use them mostly for lugging cargo up and down the Basin, but you'd think in this important case they could equip one with a temporary habitat and facilities?"

"They are failing. The air transports."

"What?"

Riveli started to pace. Amhama and Liaei stared at her with curious attention.

"It's not been generally announced so as not to generate public worry, but there have been some foodstuff delivery issues, and some water refinery shipment problems. The Basin City water purification plant had a transport crash halfway up the slope. When they examined what was left of it, the harmonium field was gone, completely lifeless. And there's nothing they can do but trash the equipment when that happens. And so," continued Riveli, "they've had to trash fifteen transports since this winter. That's an unheard of failure rate, not with harmonium-powered equipment."

"Oh, my . . ." said Amhama.

Liaei snorted. "We're all falling apart, aren't we?" she said.

"So then how do we get Liaei up there safely?"

Riveli thought for a moment. "She'll take a police patrol car. Yes, I know it is not ideally equipped to hover at such a steep angle as the Basin slope, but if going slowly, and well-fortified with emergency supplies and plenty of water, she'll be fine. In fact, the safest course is to follow the waterpipe canal and then the River all the way up the slope."

"Goodness, that might take days," Amhama said.

But Liaei spoke up. "I'd like that," she said. "I will finally get to see The River That Flows Through The Air."

❝I am all packed," Liaei announced to the harmonium. "Not that many personal items in my box, mostly datapad and audio library components and extra power packs. A couple of pretty self-decorative presents from the horticulturists and Amhama, for my fifteenth birthday. My cool weather jacket, even though it is hot here now. Extra underwear and . . . pads."

"Sounds like you are prepared," replied the harmonium.

Liaei shrugged. "Prepared for not sure what. But yes, I am."

"Then the last lesson from this node in Basin City will be about intimacy, and about fear."

"What do you mean?"

"It is a natural thing to be afraid of the unknown," said the harmonium. "And another entity, a person you have never met, is an unknown. When you come together, unless you trust that no harm will befall you, you will not be receptive. We will practice an exercise that focuses your thoughts on the calm and acceptance that might be needed at that point. First, imagine a bowl of water, smooth and placid and perfectly clear. . . ."

The next morning, in the bright amber sky glow, many of them came to see her off.

"Take good care of her, Ginadi," said Amhama, releasing Liaei from a long close embrace during which she stroked the back of Liaei's head and whispered something, while moisture ran down her face. She was speaking to the patrolman who would drive Liaei up the Basin slope. It was the same police officer who had watched the streets of the night City, stopping to wave occasionally to Amhama when she worked the various night shifts over the years. She had requested him specifically for this task, because she felt she could trust him. He was a stranger, yet familiarity was a thing of degrees. And over the many nights she had seen his calm reliable solid face from the other side of the car's security glass, Amhama sensed that she need have no fear.

Ginadi was a tall, large-built man, approximately Amhama's age, with muscled arms that showed through the fabric of his gray uniform. But ages were hard to tell, Liaei knew. They all looked gently alike, these people of a human species separate from herself.

"Don't worry," he replied, squinting in the bright morning glare of the Day God, watching Amhama with dark warm eyes. "She will be fine, I promise. The back cargo space has been converted into a rest bunk and the closet's a voidroom, and there is plenty of food and water. She can use the rear harmonium port to pass the time. Or she can watch the scenery. We'll make as many stops as necessary."

"Thank you," said Amhama. "I wish I could be there with you, but I will slow you down."

Ginadi nodded.

Liaei knew it was true because the police cruiser could not support more than two people and be remotely efficient—not with all the habitat modifications in the rear cargo area. And not when it will be climbing up a 25 degree and higher slope for most of the journey and would have to keep its tail end from bumping the uneven and sharp rock formations of the ground.

The horticulturists from the medicineal—the closest she had to a real family, Liaei realized—stood just behind Amhama. Chwanta was still wearing her sterile lab coat, since she had come directly from a night shift to see Liaei. Chwanta patted and then tousled Liaei's already longer than shoulder-length hair, and said, "You are beautiful, Queen. Remember that."

Finnei and Toliwe were next. Liaei understood that they must have discussed the significance of this gesture beforehand, because Toliwe said, "We have something for you," while at the same time Finnei proffered a small metallic gift box decorated in a bright harmonium field pattern that danced in illusory motion around the center and rotated along the box's perimeter.

"Open it later," Finnei said. "Open it when you get bored with the scenery."

I will never get bored with the scenery, Liaei wanted to retort.

But at that point Mara, the machine tech, pulled up from the back of their group and smoothly extended a limb from her chassis. It was holding a new datapad attachment. "This is an expanded memory music player, the latest model," said Mara's lively pseudo-living voice. "So that you can always dance, Liaei. It's been a pleasure!"

Liaei bit her lip, holding back something that was breaking inside of her. That except for her dear Amhama, Mara would act the most human of them all. . . .

Ginadi cleared his throat and then checked his right armband. He set a custom chronometer to start measuring at that point, which would divide their multi-day journey into appropriate rest periods. "We should be on our way."

Whoever said the Pacific Basin was only a toxic wasteland, had not been faced with the grandeur of the near upright walls of this deepest and likely most ancient of earth's planetary craters.

One had to imagine the greatest mountain range, its invisible peaks lost in a horizon line that was so far overhead that it amounted to heaven. Beyond that dissipated edge, the remaining portion of sky was all solar orange radiance, a burning atmospheric mass of deflected radiation and particles of airborne matter, a soup of pale amber cream that somehow blinded the eye.

As the police cruiser left the outskirts of Basin City, Liaei, sitting in the front passenger seat next to Officer Ginadi, stared at the receding familiar landmarks. There went the concrete water refinery domes, the tall city center with the medicineal building towering above many others, the crisscrossing network of suspended streets, suspended aqueducts, various residential and shopping complexes, everything dotted by blazing panels of light that were solar energy collectors plugged into the harmonium systems all around the city.

There, if she blinked, she could see the glare of light reflecting in the windows of the multi-floor complex where she and Amhama had lived for the past fifteen years.

And beyond everything in the receding distance of the horizon was the oil slick stripe of the Oceanus. A black metallic snake, it rested, mirroring the Day God.

Road traffic was light as usual, consisting of occasional city buses, freight transports, and personal units. They had taken the wide main street that ran alongside the grayish concrete and metal waterline, as wide in circumference as the street itself.

"See that?" said Ginadi, as they swept onward, hovering about half a meter above street level, at a precise speed and height limit for this particular city area. "Can you guess how many cubic tons of purified water it carries?"

"Hmm, I used to know this," Liaei replied. "I believe it varies seasonally, doesn't it?"

Ginadi shook his head in reproach, eyes steady on the road as he steered the two pilot rods in manual mode. "What, they don't teach you the basics in school any more? It's thirty cubic tons per hour on the average, which is pretty low volume for this pipe diameter. And yes, it varies from the low of about twenty cubic tons in the summer to a high of about forty during the highest precipitate winters."

"Sorry that I don't know this off the top of my head. And I was taught in a special school," Liaei retorted. She stared at him with a beginning frown, but then noticed lines of humor at his lips. Officer Ginadi was teasing her.

The main street and the waterline meandered past natural land structures around which they had been built, with fewer and fewer human-made structures on both sides, while the angle of the slope incline started to increase, until they left the city limits, marked by nothing other than a sign and a small border station.

As they approached the border station, Ginadi talked to them on the voice comm, and without even slowing down they were cleared to proceed. Liaei saw two officers wave at them from the rounded transparent windows in a small three story concrete tower.

Since hardly anyone ever left Basin City, they were now the only ones on the road.

On both sides of them, reddish sedimentary rock, striated layers, rust, amber, rose, teal, sienna. No earth, no soil, thought Liaei. Such was only to be found in enclosed city parks and in the greenhouses where under pristine climate-controlled conditions the horticulturists grew plantlife for food and other organic consumption.

Except for microbes in the atmospheric cocktail distributed by the winds and the almost non-existent rainfall, there was no life.

The cruiser top and windows were closed for comfort, and the air conditioning and oxygenator and humidifier were on, the comfortable mixture coming like a breath of life through the vents. Otherwise, Liaei knew, they would be bathed by very dry rarified air at this point, the kind that normally made her lightheaded and gave her a sinus headache. But at least at this distance the stink of Oceanus would be almost gone. She was not sure if that was such a good thing since in many ways the Oceanus was home. She had lived along its mineral-encrusted shoreline all her life and it was a familiar bloated monster of inky-black poison and life, a paradox.

So long, Oceanus, she thought. Then she turned around and kept her eyes on the rising way before them.

The road that had been a city street was now a faded and unmarked strip of dust-blown ashen pavement, cracked in many places, as it crawled upward only a couple of meters on the left side of the waterline.

The great water pipe itself, a monstrous concrete worm burrowing above ground, rested within circular support rings of black metal alloy. The supports were placed at regular intervals along the pipeline. They were anchored in place on the nether side by subterranean posts in the sloping ground like giant nails driven deep into the rock flesh of the Basin.

If one looked far enough overhead, the worm narrowed as it receded in the distance, slivering upward, curving occasionally, meandering along natural formations. And the support rings running along its surface appeared to be the annelid segments of the creature.

And then, at some point up the slope, the worm ended, and a line of reflected fire began.

They were about a day's travel distance from it.

Liaei watched the monotony of the sienna and rust rock coloration bathed in bright Day God glare as the world on both sides of them had become a single massive slope. As they ascended higher and higher there was a new sensation, a frequent popping pressure in her ears.

She glanced occasionally and shyly at the rather quiet Officer Ginadi next to her, who engaged the autopilot function, and now occupied himself by watching data on the harmonium display field. He looked up only to make sure they were indeed on course and hovering above the smoother safety of the ancient road and not the sharp boulders just meters away. Were the cruiser to scrape its bottom due to a miscalculation in hover altitude and angle, at least they would not attain as much damage on pavement as they would on irregular rock.

The road was ancient indeed. At one point historically, Liaei knew, people had traveled up and down it by foot, or by manually held sedan chair. No wheeled or other road-contacting vehicles were allowed, because if such a vehicle's braking mechanism failed, it would roll down out of control due to the high incline, and would cause an unpredictable amount of damage to others on the road below it. Thus, all traffic had been pedestrian.

Or maybe not, she remembered her lessons suddenly. Around the time the road was being built in various stages there had still been some domestic non-human species of animals, mostly quadruped, and they had been used as pack-animals and cargo carriers—a form of intra-species slavery.

No wonder they were now extinct. As technology developed and the world went on, nearsighted homo sapiens did not find enough value in other species and thus did not provide for them. Since, in that dawn of sentience, the health hazards of eating meat increased and compassion slowly flowered and overtook cruelty, the designation of animals as food became irrelevant. And companion animals, the few fortunate non-food species that had served the dubious purpose of pets, were also eventually left to dissipate as an unnecessary luxury in a world of dwindling resources.

They had been marvelous terrestrial aliens, Liaei thought.

We ate them, we tortured and abused them as consumable things, and we abandoned them in the end. And in all our wisdom and profundity of logic and thought we never did learn to properly value those beings, thought Liaei, those wondrous true aliens on our own planet, for their own sake—for the sake of the miracle of life that they stood for, just as much as we did. Sentience had not been enough to guide us. It had been the people of my own genetic makeup, responsible for the loss. And now, for these modern homo sapiens, who *do* know better than to use and enslave others, it is too late. These human beings live in a world where they are the only animals left. And I too, I live along with them.

And as the pavement flew by, eternally falling in an optical illusion before her eyes, Liaei imagined ghosts out of the depths of millennia, millions walking up and down that road, biped and quadruped, burdened and not, of their free will and—on behalf of someone else—without. They trudged, clad in pale cotton that covered flesh of all hues, while the Day God rose and set above them millions of times, and at the same time gradually swelled to fill most of the sky until the sky held no more ancient blue, only gold.

And the Oceanus, it had stood closer to the top edge and higher then, probably almost at this same exact point which they passed now along the slope. And there was no Basin City. . . .

"Hungry?" said Ginadi, interrupting her reverie. "Almost midday meal time."

Liaei glanced his way, nodding, then added, "Sure."

"Then let's stop for a stretch and lunch."

The cruiser had to be decelerated very carefully. And then—since in motion it had been positioned at a slight opposite angle to the slope, to correct the extreme leaning-back effect they would have had to experience otherwise—it had to be made parallel to the slope, and then the hover altitude was diminished as it gently plastered itself closer and closer against the road.

Liaei and Ginadi were nearly lying back in their chairs when the cruiser finally slipped to a stop and its parking grip-supports were extended to attach to the pavement.

The air systems turned off and the doors came open with a slight hiss, then warm and thin air came to engulf them. It beat at Liaei's face with shocking impact, tangling her hair.

"We're sitting in the middle of the road," she said.

"Right," said the officer in his usual calm voice, with a touch of humor. "You think anyone would mind that we're blocking their way?"

Liaei laughed.

But then he added, "Careful, by the way, if you're afraid of heights. As you stand up and get out of the car, move slowly, and don't look back immediately. Get a feel for the ground first."

He wasn't kidding. As Liaei got out of the cruiser, she was buffeted by the dry wind and an immediate overpowering vertigo. She remembered the gym back at Basin City, how the aerial exercises made her weak and faint in the pit of her stomach at first, and how she breathed to control the terror.

Breathing deeply in a similar fashion, she stood up, the non-slip soles of her shoes gripping the road. And then slowly she turned around, extending her arms at both sides a little way, for natural balance.

An impossible vista was before her.

The world was falling away into a rust-orange haze, dissolving in the distance.

Down, down, down.

All perspective lines receded. Rocks that were huge boulders and cliffsides, when they passed by, appeared tiny handfuls of pebbles far below. The paved road behind the cruiser was a stripe that slipped away along the pipe waterline, curved occasionally, and disappeared in the incalculable distance, narrowing to a point.

They were now too far to see Basin City or even the Oceanus, in the atmospheric haze.

Liaei had grown so light and weightless and bereft of anchor that she knew that if she were to take another step down the road, she would fall, then roll down the slope forever. . . .

With a force of will Liaei swallowed to loosen the constriction in her throat, then turned her back on the road. As a result of her movement she heard tiny pebbles crunch under her feet, then heard them clatter and roll away, down, down, down. . . .

Inside the cruiser, Ginadi was making a call to the City, to report on their progress. He was talking with his mouth full, holding a half-eaten pre-packaged vegetable roll sandwich in one hand, and gesticulating with the other as he attempted to describe something about hover propulsion to the party on the other end of the harmonium link. He stopped only to offer Liaei another sandwich, a small jar of creamy white dipping sauce, and a chilled drink container.

Liaei ate, then went to the back to use the tiny voidroom, lingered for a moment next to her spare luggage rack, wondering if she should open the gift box from Toliwe and Finnei. But no, she was not bored yet. And she was somehow unwilling to find out what it contained. And so she returned to the front seat.

Ginadi ended the call and they were once again on their way.

While the Day God continued its cycle in the sky, toward late afternoon, they had stopped twice more, and soon it would be dark. With the approach of twilight and falling away of bright light, the colors gold and orange rust began to fade, while the Basin walls darkened and deep browns and blues took the place of ambers. With the departure of focus, Liaei was nodding off, hypnotized by the relentless optical illusion of the falling road.

They finally stopped for the night when the road was completely dark and only the twin rows of five headlights of the cruiser cut through the ebony thickness of night.

"We could keep going, but it is no longer as safe," said Ginadi, landing them smoothly. "And you are far too important to risk."

"What about you?" asked Liaei in a sleepy voice, unable to repress a smile.

"Me? I'm terribly important, of course. But I am not going to be the Queen of the Hourglass like you, kid," he said. "Now, off to the back, with you. Get some rest for tomorrow. Oh, and here's an extra sandwich. Chew—helps to clear out the pressure in your ears."

"Can we please have some tea first?"

He grumbled about demanding Queens and heating water at this hour, but then, grinning, rummaged in their supply bag, and plugged in the small water pot.

Liaei got her hot soothing mug and took it with her to sip as she got comfortable in the strange narrow bunk bed.

When she finally slept, she dreamt of an Oceanus full of aromatic tea, and on its surface were floating ancient temporal devices, clocks and hourglasses and bits of unknown machinery, half submerged in warm amber liquid that all started running down an endless downhill slope.

In the morning, what woke Liaei was the sound of the wind. It was buffeting the parked cruiser on all sides, howling in gusts, whistling, and in the background stood a constant low hum. She never realized how different this humming silence was, a thousand meters above Basin City, how much movement and tonality it contained.

Ginadi was napping in the front, his large uniformed frame stretched out along the two front seats. He grunted and got up as soon as Liaei moved into the front, and grumbled again, then opened the outside doors to her, saying "Careful, all right?"

While Ginadi used the facilities in the back, Liaei stood just outside on the pavement, stomping her feet and stretching after a strange cramped night. She had gotten used to the extreme slope and was no longer as dizzy when looking at the grand vista below.

The Day God had barely risen, and a large portion of the slope overhead was still in shadow, while off on the horizon opposite, the world was already in orange reflected flame.

The air was a bit more chilly at this altitude and had not warmed up yet, so that Liaei, wearing no jacket and only a thin t-shirt and long pants, felt goosebumps along her arms. But it was a strange invigorating sensation, a wildness in her lungs, as she breathed the rarified air and spread her arms wide, and watched the precipice below the slope fill with rich creamy light.

They got going once again, and this time Liaei looked at the roadway before them and noticed suddenly how much closer the line of fire was that indicated the end of the waterpipe and the beginning of The River That Flows Through The Air.

"How long till we are up close to it?" she whispered in reverence.

Officer Ginadi thought for a moment, checking their progress on his bulky chronometer. "I'd say middle of the afternoon. You really want to see it, don't you?"

"Oh, Day God, yes. I've been wanting to see it ever since I knew that it was there to be seen."

Looking ahead at the moving road, Ginadi smiled.

Nothing could have prepared her.
        As they drew closer, the stripe of razor light grew closer, aligning itself with the end of the winding waterpipe, becoming a distant extension of it, becoming thicker, brighter.

And yet, nothing the mind could visualize beforehand was even remotely close.

By lunchtime, Liaei felt herself growing tense, as she retreated deeply into her seat, staring intently ahead, staring at it in the dwindling distance. Muscles of her neck and shoulders were tightening, clenched internally, expectation gnawing at her. She wasn't even hungry and wanted to refuse the food offered her, but the officer insisted, and so she chewed something that was as exciting as dust to her single-minded focused senses. Chewed, as she watched it, always bright and coming more and more into focus, yet always just out of reach of comprehension.

Finally, as the imaginary center point of the Day God stood nearly in perfect zenith overhead, covering the sky with golden orange radiance, they had climbed high enough so that Liaei could see the edge of the waterpipe as it ended about two hundred meters above them up the slope. . . .

"We'll stop now so that you can see," said Ginadi, aware of her intensity.

Liaei did not answer immediately, she was so clenched. Then she nodded.

The cruiser decelerated and Liaei watched the last dozen support rings flash past them along the gray concrete of the water pipe surface.

As they slowed and lost hover altitude, there was an approaching roar up ahead. They could hear it through the closed windows of the cruiser, a sound rising above the constant wind hum.

The cruiser doors shot open, and Liaei stepped outside, followed by Ginadi, with his usual, "Be careful now, okay? Watch your step."

Liaei stared, her eyes drying from not blinking for so long.

Just ahead, the angle of slope showed her the topside curvature of the concrete pipe as it ended, and beyond it she heard the waterfall roar of escaping water, but did not quite see it, not from this low angle, not just yet.

"Watch your step, slowly now." Ginadi, again.

Liaei walked uphill, mesmerized, toward the curving concrete visible edge, toward the roar on the other side.

And then suddenly, the angle of the slope and her proximity allowed her to see.

A three-dimensional wall of water, transparent and clear, with only a shadow tint of reflected sky orange, as seen *through* it.

A wall of water, even and smooth, bursting through, out of the shadowed darkness of the pipe, out of its long containment of concrete, and rushing up.

Up along the slope, into the air.

Day God shining through it, its glory scattering, diffracting, splintering, fragmenting into shards, as though seen through a wall of moving faceted crystal, a sheet of variegated living liquid glass.

Liaei took another step or two, up the paved road, until she stood a meter away from the edge of the pipe, its gaping circumference balanced on the last support ring that just protruded about half a meter out of the ground. She looked down and saw that the rocks immediately below it were different from the ruddy barren stonescape all around. They were dark with moisture, dark with greenish discoloration of algae growth. Slippery, smooth-polished, they glistened, as they might have a million years ago when the Oceanus waters would have submerged them.

Smooth, they were, polished by the million-year continued erosion caused by mere water spray. While all around, the dry rocks had undergone an opposite kind of erosion—once smooth beneath the water, they were now carved, grated, and sharpened by the abrasive sand particles and wind.

And then Liaei realized she felt a difference against her face, the pores of her skin, a coolness in the air—the wet spray. It was as though she were standing with her face against a humidifier unit.

Except this moisture was in the air itself, for many meters in the surrounding area.

"Amazing, isn't it?" Ginadi's voice came from behind. "They still don't know what mechanism makes the water flow up like that, without mechanized pressurization. Just look at it, it is flowing smoothly, slowly even. Like a sheet of glass sliding up."

"Yes . . ." said Liaei. She never took her eyes off the flow. "Could it be a force opposite of the earth's pull? Or maybe a displacement of tiny sub-particles to make the water molecules change physical state temporarily so that they become weightless and can be made to go up, or something?"

"Or something," said Ginadi. "No one knows. Not even the harmonium knowledge base. We just know it is an amazingly neat trick, and wish we could copy it."

"Could it be an illusion of the eye?" said Liaei.

"Nope," Ginadi said. "It's real, kid. Real water flowing up. We draw the sludge out of the Oceanus, put the purified stuff into the pipe end down in Basin City refinery, and it just comes up here. And keeps on going. Been that way for as long as we can remember."

"Do you think maybe I can stick my hand in it to make sure?"

He laughed. "I am sure it's been done before. But probably you shouldn't, since they'll have my hide down in the City for putting you into any unnecessary risk situation, and this one's a definite unknown. Why don't you look instead at how the water continues moving up, there, just ahead? Let's walk a bit farther along so that you can see."

They walked with slow very careful paces, and Liaei watched the bizarre sheet of water at least three meters thick (she guessed by its level of transparency) and who knew how wide climb alongside her up the slope. Then slowly it rose even higher in a gradually up-curving arc that was departing the angle of the Basin slope. As it finally leveled out, the moving wall of water lay at least thirty meters up in the air like a curtain of liquid molded light through which the Day God was distorted and pulled askew, bent into new directions. . . .

It was akin to a transparent bridge standing overhead, Liaei realized suddenly, and she could probably walk right underneath it and stare at the Day God broken up as though in a kaleidoscope toy.

And then, in the distance interval of several car lengths Liaei saw the first support pillar.

"What is that?" she asked, but then realized that this was the same type of black metallic support ring as had held in place the water pipe earlier, and that it was somehow continuing to "hold" together the water of The River that Flows Through The Air. Except, this support ring seemed taller and it extended out farther from the sloping ground, with its circular band portion about twenty meters in the air.

Water flowed through the center of the ring and onward to the next support ring in the same interval distance, and so on, until it again disappeared into a fiery thread up-slope.

"Again, we don't know," said Ginadi. "It's like it is guiding the water somehow, from ring to ring."

"What are those pillars made of?"

"Some kind of metal alloy, I believe the harmonium analyzed it as such."

"Oh, Day God! How does it work?" Liaei exclaimed in a burst of frustration. She watched the bridge of water that was now high overhead, belted with the strange containment rings. Its roar was barely diminished but the microscopic spray stood in the air, softening the rocks directly below which seemed painted with a moist shadow.

Without asking permission this time, Liaei approached the closest rock and placed a fingertip along its sleek surface. It came away slippery and likely coated with invisible life.

"All right, I think we've seen enough, so let's be on our way," said Ginadi immediately, giving her a brief concerned glance.

"I am sure it's non-toxic."

"Right, well, still. You can watch the River as we drive right next to it all the way up."

The rest of the afternoon was monotonous and a kind of disoriented haze. Once the cruiser gained hover altitude, they were only about halfway up between the River and the paved roadway, and Liaei watched the water's glittering mass and surface, at times appearing transparent, and at others, molten fire, depending on the angle of their parallel movement.

Liaei stared at it constantly—through it, and at it, and around it—until the glittering line of reflected fire imprinted upon her retinas even when she looked away for brief moments. In her field of vision the River image was pasted like a white snake against the reddish rocks.

Liaei remembered them taking another rest stop and chewing more prepackaged food for dinner at some point. And then, as darkness of evening slowly approached, the transparent water took on strange blue-greenish hues, and it left a deeper shadow upon the rocks below.

With the coming of night, the River at last disappeared, blending into the darkness of sky. They parked the cruiser on a strip of pavement, and ate, then slept, and this time Liaei remembered having no dreams, only an image of a stripe of flowing white fire.

The following day was to be the last of their journey. They were to reach the uppermost edge of the Basin slope and emerge onto the earth's Plateau surface by the middle of the afternoon.

Liaei spent the time not listening to music, not checking out her harmonium entertainment modules in the port in the back, but just looking outside the window in a self-induced stupor. Sometimes she counted the seconds that passed between the appearance of the support ring posts that flashed outside the window like dark upright shadows. At other times she tried to see an infinitesimal difference between the hue of the water as it entered each new stretch of segment between each ring. Sometimes it seemed to stand still, then flow wildly forward; sometimes it was all clear and transparent cream-orange, at other times there would be just a hint of green, then blue, then a bit of violet. She knew it had to be the prismatic effect of refracted light. But it was still fun to watch for different colors of the rainbow appear here and there, like wondrous surprises.

About two more rest stops, and without realizing it—since she was so busy staring at the flowing water to the side of her— the horizon defined by the slope was coming down lower and lower ahead of them, closer and closer. It no longer seemed halfway up the sky, but was now just the height of a tall mountain.

And in the course of mid-afternoon, the edge seemed to draw so close up ahead that Liaei could reach out and touch it.

"Almost there," said Ginadi. He glanced at her. "You excited?"

Liaei nodded.

He grinned. "If that's your way of being excited. . . . Nah."

But then he pointed with his finger to the quickly approaching upper edge of the horizon. "See that bright dot of light, just to the right of where the River seems to disappear over the top? That is the border patrol tower of Edge City."

"I see it. Neat!"

But Ginadi was already calling ahead, to discuss their approach.

Liaei again looked at the wall of water at their side, ever rushing by, transparent yet filled with hidden or implied color.

Then it happened.

They were out of the Basin suddenly, for the horizon fell away completely at their feet, and suddenly the cruiser was straightening to match the curve-and-then-flattening of the roadway.

They hung in the air at the edge of a grand flatland the size of the whole world. The earth was bathed in gold, all orange, amber, rust. It was pale and uniform.

Everything impossible, flat.

There, like a stalagmite growth from the cliffside stood the gray concrete tower, swept featureless by the daylight, almost the twin of the one down in Basin City.

And then Liaei glanced to the right of her. She observed how The River That Flows Through The Air also curved along an imaginary line and straightened out, water running from ring to ring, and on into the endless distance.

Beyond it, rising in many shapes of pale and dark concrete and metal, was Edge City.

"I'm to take you directly to the Palace of the Clock King," said Ginadi. He noticed Liaei's dazed, frozen expression, as though she was still submerged in a multi-day dream state.

"Okay," Liaei said in a dull voice, as their cruiser started to move away from the edge of the Plateau surface. Onward it swept, reducing its hover altitude and speed for the city limits, past the guard tower into this alien city of pale brilliant surfaces that looked not all that different than the one she had called home for the last fifteen years.

Except, there were more people on the streets here, moving energetically, their skin shades ranging from palest alabaster to deep bronze, smooth heads gleaming, dressed in brighter clothes, with more fashion variety than the jeans and fiber t-shirt that was the most commonly seen outfit in the Basin. Pedestrians walked along newer sidewalks of solid well-cared-for pavement which was not upraised from the ground itself but smoothed right on top of it.

"The ground is firm here, unlike down where we came from," Ginadi mentioned, seeing the direction of her stare. Remember that we're on the normal surface level now, just like most of the earth—none of that sedimentary crumbling stuff. This is all mostly solid rock."

Liaei continued looking.

"How are your ears?"

"Fine. A little stuffed."

"It'll clear up fast enough as your body gets used to the different pressure." And then he added, "The name of the chief nurse is Vioma, by the way. She is the horticulturist medic who is waiting to see you. She just told me she is very happy to finally meet you."

"Yes," Liaei said. "Chief nurse Riveli told me."

"Tired?"

"Yes. But I am okay, really, thank you. This is very interesting, this city."

Ginadi smiled. "Don't be too scared now. We're going to the cultural center of this place, the so-called Palace of the Clock King. There's all kinds of neat stuff there, museums, libraries, theaters, performance arenas. Even that River of yours, you know it flows right past the Palace courtyard? See, we're still following it, even now."

And as Liaei turned to glance off to the side, about three street blocks away, she saw the gleaming fire of it, the living moving transparent entity. It appeared and disappeared beyond buildings and city structures, a glittering worm.

"Where does it go?" she asked. "I mean, where does it end?"

Ginadi wrinkled his smooth bronze browline. "I'm not sure. Never thought to ask. Sorry, don't know. I've been to Edge City a couple dozen times but never followed the River much farther than here and there. You need to ask the locals."

The Palace was recognizable in the distance, even to someone who had no idea what to look for.

It was a vaguely dome-shaped circular structure of deep gray-rose granite stone, a work of ancient art. As they approached through city traffic, Liaei noticed that it was in fact a circular pyramid of expanding platforms, like great stepping-stones in a circular staircase. The floors, ever narrowing in diameter toward the center, were often enhanced by regular columns, and there were many windows of modern plasti-glass and glassoid material. They shone like mosaic panels from a distance. At the center of the Palace stood a tall thin needle-tower of several hundred floors, the tallest structure in the city. At its tip was a harmonium-powered antenna that could broadcast into the atmosphere and beyond.

Liaei gasped in wonder, seeing it. She had been taught in her schooling that this was the oldest structure known to the moderns, a remainder from the dawn of the harmonium civilization.

But she had no idea it was part of the Palace where she was now headed. Or maybe, at some point she did, but she had paid no attention in class, had forgotten. . . .

And now it was drawing near, a titan alone in a flat world, and the Palace structures were emerging in places all around them, drawing them in, engulfing.

Another couple of minutes, and they arrived.

Vioma was a petite tiny woman dressed in a sterile mauve lab coat, completely unimposing, completely unlike Riveli. And yet she had energetic eyes, unusual to Liaei who was so used to measured softness and a kind of dissipated lack of focus in the eyes of all the people who comprised her limited world.

Vioma met them outside the front entrance of the Palace, where Ginadi stopped his cruiser and several strangers came out to begin helping them unload Liaei's meager baggage items.

"Let me look at you, Liaei!" Vioma exclaimed, staring unabashedly at Liaei's deep gold hair gathered in a thick tail at the back, at her brows, the curves of her form. "Oh, you are wonderful, just lovely, child! They did so well with you, in Basin City."

And then Vioma corrected herself. "Not a child for much longer of course, since the Ceremony is scheduled for the coming week."

"The Ceremony?" Liaei said. Then she understood. "Oh, yes, of course. Nice to meet you, Vioma, and I look forward to the detailed last minute training. I have a general idea of it, of course—"

Vioma shook the palm of her hand. "Not here, Liaei. We can talk of all this after you've settled into your apartment and rested up a bit. Today you move in, tomorrow we run a couple of last minute physical tests, then we train. All right?"

"Good," said Ginadi, who in that moment got out of the cruiser. "Because the poor kid is barely keeping awake, she's so tired. Go easy on her."

"Thank you for all your help on the trip, Officer Ginadi," said Liaei.

But he only smiled, then reached out and unexpectedly patted her on the top of her head.

"Always a pleasure. Now, you take care, girl! Remember what I say, always be careful when you walk up a slope, all right?"

And then with a wink and a nod he retreated back into the cruiser, and was on his way. With his departure the last bit of familiarity left Liaei. She was now truly away from home.

Or maybe not quite.

Liaei glanced up once as they were heading indoors, and saw a familiar razor-gleam of clean transparent water rushing suspended through the air, just around the corner of the Palace building.

"The Clock King," Vioma said. "How much did they tell you about him?"

"Not that much. I mostly asked the harmonium a million leading questions, so I have some idea that he is my biological mate."

Liaei was seated in a comfortable chair in a room with a tall airy ceiling and walls decorated with pleasing warm earth tones. Across from her in another chair sat Vioma. They were both holding warm mugs of slightly sweet saffron tea. On a small glass table between them stood a decanter and a tray of fresh hothouse fruits and baked goods.

"His story is an ancient puzzle." Vioma took a sip, then licked her austere lips with the tip of her tongue. "The Clock King has been here, or rather, has been discovered here, in this structure of the early harmonium age, by the earlier generations."

Liaei nodded.

"He is within a device which maintains him in a biological suspended state. The function of that device is also unclear, but we do know how to bring him back to us. And we've been reviving him periodically over the years."

"I see," Liaei said.

"Your task is indeed to be there when the Clock King is revived, greet him and become comfortable with him, and mate with him. Don't be afraid, he knows exactly what is expected of him, and much of the ritual is in fact to facilitate your acquaintance and give you time before the resulting biological mating act."

"How will we speak?" Liaei asked. "His language must be ancient and different."

Vioma smiled. "Good question. The device which contains him will prepare him somehow. He will speak and understand—at least our records show that he always does."

"Records?"

"You may see them later. They are rather old document files that the harmonium stored for the last several generations. They will give you some idea. But—actually, no, I don't think you need to see them just yet. Nothing terribly important, but just so as not to have preconceptions when you meet him."

"Oh . . ." said Liaei, thinking that Vioma was being evasive. "Is there something about him that will disturb me?"

But Vioma put her mug down and leaned forward, closer. "No, I think you will be just fine."

Liaei was becoming very cold suddenly. True realization, an awakening to the full implications of what was about to happen to her, made her as numb as though she was back somewhere along the Basin slope, looking down over the abyss.

Except, this abyss was even less familiar, less comprehensible.

"Okay . . ." she said softly. "Does the Clock King have a human name?"

On the day of the Ceremony, Liaei was taken to a strange bathing area the like of which she had never seen. Whereas normally everyone would shower in a cube closet with a timed high-pressure spray of rationed water, here was a generous basin the size of a bed, filled with precious water. The water was scented with some kind of flower and herb essence, and had a fine oily film that sparkled. She was told to enter and submerge herself in the warm water and stay there for as long as her skin needed to be soothed and lubricated and acquire a sheen.

When Liaei came out, her damp hair plastered to her in long curling strands, holding a large absorbent towel around herself, she was in a chamber filled with colors and scents. Two appearance professionals greeted her, and they worked on her, drying and brushing her hair so that it lay soft and shining down her back, then applied adult makeup on her face.

Liaei thought of the suave women in the dance clubs who had colorful designs painted on the skin of their face and head and arms, with color and sparkle cosmetics. She also thought of the funny old porno displays the harmonium had shown her—the big, puffy red lips of the ancient women.

Her outfit was lying ready for her on a side table. It was a white diaphanous gown of lightweight, translucent material which reached below her ankles and swept on the floor. Underneath she was supposed to wear an odd looking halter for her breast area, and something that looked like a pair of underwear pants. The items were made of shiny metallic stretch-fabric, colored delicate bronze and gold and patterned with complex designs of various shades of deep brown. Colorful faceted faux jewel stones encrusted the belt area, and fine metallic jewelry chains hung in looping clusters, brushing against her thighs with a fringe of cold sensation.

Liaei said nothing when putting this on. She slipped the halter around her front and it fit uncomfortably around her rounded breasts, pushing them together to create a crevice. Then one of the assistants came around from the back and showed her how to clasp the thing together, and it bit into her ribcage.

The pants were slipped on next, tight against her bare skin, and the belt was low against her hips, below her exposed navel.

"Stop for a moment," said an appearance professional, as Liaei took hold of the white outer gown. "We are going to put a whole lot of traditional antique jewelry on you."

The appearance professional brought forward a large box and inside, Liaei saw sparkling decorative costume pieces made of stones, metallic chains, odd pretty shapes, carved, molded, faceted, rounded.

"I don't suppose your earlobes are pierced?"

Liaei shook her head.

"Then we'll use loops that go over the ear and hang beneath. Now, put out your hands."

Liaei did, and several moments later, was burdened.

Metal bands circled around her wrists and upper arms, rings stifled her fingers, various lengths of loops of metal and stones were strung together around her neck. Symmetrical looped bunches of jewelry went around and over her ears. Finally, a band of metal, a torque, was placed around her forehead and the back of her head, horizontal and just above her browline. In the center of the torque a suspended brilliant jewel of deep amber rested in the cradle between her brows like a third eye.

"Now, the outer gown. It will come off, as you approach the Clock King."

"So I get to greet him in underwear," said Liaei.

"Oh, no, no! This is an ancient traditional costume of seduction. Trust me, he will love you in it!" The appearance professional laughed, and Liaei wondered if the person was a man or a woman, since he or she was glam-dressed to the point of obscurity.

"Now, just a final touch-up of facial paint around the eyes, and you are ready to go! What a gorgeous exotic creature!"

Minutes later, they were done with her at last.

When Vioma came to fetch her, also dressed in her finest, Liaei was an unreal, sparkling, jeweled, veiled statue with dark glass eyes.

In the monolithic Palace central hall that could hold thousands, a mere handful of people gathered—all of them horticulturist techs, medics, and other scientists.

In the center, upraised on a sort of stone dais, was a strange mechanical device. It was circular and flat, about a meter in height, and six meters in diameter and the topside of it was bisected by many radii that came from the exact center and out, in even intervals. The edges along the circumference of the device were marked in archaic symbols that Liaei recognized as an ancient form of symbolic recording, a numeric decimal code of combinations of linear, angular, and circular strokes. They were impressed onto the metallic surface of the device, pale metal against dark deep brown, near-black. Several arrows of various lengths overlay the device like radii extending from the middle. There were at least ten of them, and they were all movable around the small palm-sized hub in the center.

The thing was a clock. An ancient time measuring device. Except, Liaei realized, as she stood on the platform before it, this one was a monstrous, somehow useless thing. She imagined the network of interlocking gears of all diameter sizes and coiled tension springs underneath its dark metallic face. And somewhere, among the cold sharp parts of angular metal, he was imprisoned, the Clock King.

He was inside, waiting for her.

Two of the scientists in the foreground stepped forward and started to wind the arrows on the face of the Clock. They aligned them in precise order next to various symbols on the outer border, along the faint concentric circles that Liaei only now noticed were etched on the surface. A third tech assisted by holding down combinations of several recessed buttons that were along the outer edge, as various motions were carried out by the other two.

Vioma drew closer to Liaei and took her cold right hand in her own, only slightly more living one. "They are setting time the old fashioned way," she whispered in a comforting tone of voice. "It's based upon the very first harmonium calendar which we no longer use. It's certainly not the oldest known to humanity, but it is the closest that makes sense to this device. Took them several decades to figure that out."

Liaei listened in silence.

"When they are done, we will hear the clockwork mechanism come to life. We will wait for the cycle to end, and the Clock King will emerge. At that point it will be time for you to proceed as discussed. Are you ready?"

Liaei nodded.

The last arrow hand was aligned, and all those standing in the hall heard a rumbling hum. The sound came to life from nothing and built on a very low frequency, until its echo made the floor and walls vibrate.

Liaei felt herself lightheaded, faint, sick to her stomach. The bright illumination in the hall made all things appear washed out, pale, and her mouth was dry, while all the rings, bracelets and chains lying like armor against her cold skin began to constrict—an illusion of pressure was building.

The hum grew, rising in frequency, and then became recognizable as rhythmic grating of gears, moving parts aligning, something happening on the inside.

For long interminable moments the whole world was vibrating, humming, contorting. The Clock was a monster coming to life, contracting and expanding its innards. Then, suddenly, the Clock began to rise. As it came up a meter off the ground, there were metallic arms revealed in a recess underneath. They extended, gradually bringing the device to an inclined position, and then completely upright.

The Clock stood up on its edge, a single point of its diameter resting against a portion of the recessed floor—what was down there, below, in the murk, Liaei could not tell.

The Clock stood. The rhythmic hum had become high-pitched and gentle, like droplets of water hitting a filled bowl.

It was ticking.

The hands on its face made several turns around the face, and one by one they all stopped on the topmost notch symbol marked against the border. They were pointing directly up.

When the last shortest radius hand came to a stop in the upright position, the ticking stopped.

There was a moment of perfect silence.

And then the face of the clock separated from the body and fell forward and out and down—without a sound.

An inner compartment was revealed.

Within the compartment was a man. He was like a life-size toy, a statue colored blue—no, colored rose, or maybe he was black—but no, the surface of his skin was shimmering, iridescent, light waves passing over him.

The play of strange light stopped. The skin underneath was dark olive, almost with a greenish tint. His head had dark hair, and his browline too was covered with hair. He moved then, at first like a doll, then with fluid, living, albeit slow movements.

The Clock King stepped out of his chamber, and stood before them, nude and alien and unreal. His eyes were pale, possibly colorless. His shoulders were significantly wide and top-heavy compared to his hips; his body musculature well-defined. Between his thighs, his genitals were prominent, belonging to homo sapiens from ages past, and just above was a growth of dark hair, a patch.

Liaei did not stare at it as she stepped forward. Instead she looked at his beautiful impassive face, that of a stranger, as she walked the several steps, pausing when they were face to face and she could, if she wanted, embrace him.

With a slow fluid gesture that she practiced a number of times, Liaei slipped off from her shoulders the white gown that was made to separate in the middle, and she offered it to the man before her.

"Welcome, Clock King, to our time." Her voice rang out in the hall. "I am the Queen of the Hourglass."

As instructed, Liaei smiled, feeling the quivering nervous tension in her jaw. Still holding the white cloth she sank to the floor, sweeping her hands forward in a dramatic gesture of offering, and gently inclining her head. Her mane of hair followed her motion. It spilled about her shoulders, fanning out like liquid gold.

It was the hair that he observed as he took the cloth and immediately bound it around his hips, covering himself in the front.

Liaei recalled that the ancients found nudity of that portion of the body a public shame.

And then, like a shock out of the primeval ages, she heard his voice. It was deep and low, rich unlike any modern male voice she ever heard.

"When and where . . . is this?" the Clock King said.

— 2 —

The Clock

I t amused him in a small pointless way that everyone came
here to see The River That Flows Through The Air, and not
himself, the Clock King, the one and only oddity of his kind.
Actually, no, that was nonsense on all counts. They all came to
the Palace on their own business which had nothing to do with
him or his nature, or the River, but with the daily course of their
own lives. And he was not unique—not while there was *she*.

The Clock King stood on the fifth story balcony and
watched the sheet of water flow, sparkling in the orange
sunlight, jetting past just at the level of his knees. It flowed
higher off the surface, here on the Palace grounds, the aqueduct
support rings that focused it being exposed to a greater degree,
thrusting far into the air. A clever design, having it pass by his
living complex.

He could observe it this, endless and hypnotic in its joyous
flow, a striated brushstroke of hueless liquid suspended against a
warm background of nothing, and through which he could see
the horizon line.

What a strange sky it had been when he first came outside,
afterwards, after all that initial foolish ceremony. He stood,
gasping internally at the sight of the bloated giant sun that

greeted him. The sky held no blue at all, only a hint at the outermost edges. He felt the weight of it all, overpowering the mind—a mind still covered in veils of recent memory suppression, or maybe loss. . . . For, as always upon first awakening, he would forget all about the swollen sun, forget that he had seen it before in a similar engorged state for at least a hundred earlier awakenings and could observe its gradual progress into gianthood, if only memory has served him.

The second shock had been the view over the precipice of the Pacific Basin, a dry crater, with some remaining sludge they all referred to as the Oceanus, supposedly somewhere down there, hidden in the rusty haze. They had taken him there, to the edge, the same day in a hover vehicle, since he had insisted. He always did that upon first awakening, to get his immediate bearings on the world.

All along, she had been there, at his side. The Queen of the Hourglass, his manufactured mate. He observed an initial subdued silence, a shy, terrified, and complacent manner.

And so terribly young. She must have been in her teens.

The girl appeared resigned, and yet he could read the strength of her reservations despite her outward subtlety.

The current dialect of their speech came easy and musical to him, as his linguistic lobes had been prepped before he even emerged. Her name was "Liaei," and he mouthed it silently now, out of nowhere, pronouncing each vowel separately as she had done, a word with four syllables.

And his name? She had asked him, but for some reason the cotton-putty mind heaviness came to him at that point, and he realized that the systems have engaged mental suppression. Either that or he honestly did not remember his own name or whether he even had one.

Not that it mattered, here and now.

He had only one function that mattered to them, and it was the virile act of studding of their dying species. If he managed it with that golden beautiful creature—herself a fortunate anomaly—then the moderns could be assured of more viable genetic variety in the resulting child's DNA. They would take it greedily and add it to the dilute weakened geno-material in their hothouse lab stores. It would buy them several more viable generations before the genetic apathy returned.

It always did.

And he would let it happen, somehow, as always. As always, they valued him too much to forcibly take his sperm by medical means, because if his body were to be damaged, then there would be no next chance for them in the future.

The Clock King wore a shirt and jeans they had given him, and the wind tousled his longish dark brown hair. Now that he was out of suspension, he felt the beginnings of stubble on his cheeks, and would need a shave eventually. The meal he'd had, sharing it in a small cozy chamber with his Queen, consisted of a vegetarian high protein series of dishes, from plants grown by the horticulturists—their role was more important than he first imagined in this society, since they were behind the technology of all living production.

The sterile wind blew a gust of living spray from the River into his face. A strange contrast of dry and wet.

He took a step back, as though it had been a slap of reason, focusing him. And he retreated into the spacious rest chamber they had given him.

He would need all the rest he could get since tonight they would expect him to perform his function.

In a few hours, when the evening came, he would go to her.

His Queen of the Hourglass.

But now, for a short time, he was free.

— 3 —

Common Time

He comes to her or maybe she comes to him.

Most of the room is the color of amber from the light of the hundreds of old-fashioned candles, even though he knows they are not real wax and she knows they are not hothouse-born. But the ceiling is high, and it recedes in a gradual flow into deep mahogany shadow. The floor is obscured by layers of plush carpets of deep browns, greens, and rusts, patterned with pleasing intricacy.

Scent of floral and organic incense fills the air of the chamber, billowing up in thin vapor streamlets from the small corner holders.

He does not like incense, and neither does she. But neither one knows the other's preference for clean air, and thus the scent lingers, unchecked, possibly infused with aphrodisiac.

Eventually it clouds their thoughts. It is meant to do thus all along.

He comes and sits down on the great Chair which is, as always, the place of the Clock King. Its back is tall and softened for comfort, while the seat is wide and soft also, well-padded and upholstered in natural fabric. The Chair has been made to withstand repeated bodily impact in comfort.

She is frightened, but hides it well.

He is remote and hides it well.

He sits quietly, knowing the ritual from the countless other times he had participated in it. He watches her moving, as he had watched so many before her, pale or dark, large or petite, thin or rotund. She approaches him, hips swaying like a trained snake, observing the effect she has on him in what she believes to be the deepening color of his eyes, while from somewhere in the back comes the sound of music with a rhythmic beat.

She breathes deeply and tries to imagine a bowl of water, smooth and placid and perfectly clear.

He watches the young, presumably fertile body before him, breasts moving naturally in the confines of the halter, hips covered with tight jewel-encrusted fabric and a precious stone and filigree gold rosette placed in the recess of her navel.

Candlelight flares in her navel with each movement.

She is dancing for him and he acknowledges her efforts by letting his gaze slide over her body, as expected. She sees his intense, unblinking gaze and wonders if he is intoxicated by the thick air or her own self.

As she dances, she comes closer, coming down to rest on the pillow dais before the Chair, and he is again gifted with the display of golden hair cascading forward and brushing his bare knees and thighs and his feet. In such a manner she could be drying his feet with her hair like the ancient sacred whore—he cannot remember what legend that is from, but it flickers momentarily out of the past's precipice.

Up close she smells of a combination of fresh cosmetics and slightly musty costume fabric—he realizes her traditional outfit is very old, and now that he thinks about it, he remembers seeing it before, on an earlier Queen.

As the music grows more urgent, she continues swaying back and forth, side to side, as she kneels before him. Her arms are very flexible and he finds them rotund and pliant and capable, as she makes delicate gestures and draws figures in the air. At some point she puts her hands behind her, and undoes the clasp of her halter.

He sees an instant of despair in her eyes, in a single glimmer of candlelight, but then it is gone, as his focus is redirected, because her breasts come forward, bouncing slightly from being freed, button nipples protruding—and he focuses there. The halter falls down her shoulders.

She continues moving to the music, and now that he is focused on her body, she puts the tips of her fingers against him, letting them slither down his chest, the whole of his torso.

He feels something.

She is unsure if he does, but she proceeds, and a sheen of sweat is beading her skin, from the overload of her own mind.

Her hands are warm and palms somewhat moist, and she is shaking slightly as she fumbles with the wrapping of his loincloth.

He watches silently as she unwraps him, letting the silky cloth fall on both sides of him, notices the curve of her back as she sways forward then back again.

She sees that his genitals are limp and quiet. This is the moment she had been trained for all her life. And so she picks up the bowl of unguent that is sitting on the floor next to the chair, and after dipping fingertips inside, she touches him *there*, for the first time.

He feels a familiar pang, a shock of sensation, and his genitals come alive, despite himself.

It is always thus.

Drawing warm, moist, lubricated hands the full length of his crotch and down to the thick blunt tip of him, she massages him in gentle strokes.

Blood is drawn down and he hardens.

Her ears are ringing with a rush—maybe from kneeling for so long, maybe from something else.

He knows that it is time to make contact with her also, but lingers, putting it off just yet, for his mind is momentarily in an ancient daze. Close your eyes, dear, and think of England—he has no concept of what England is, but the thought is an amusing non sequitur. Again, the tumble of clouds in his mind.

Her head comes down meanwhile, the radiant gold hair covering his lap, and he feels her moist lips, then a slightly abrasive tongue, drawing him, feeding upon him, lapping at him, and it makes him shudder.

He tenses up, full body, and knowing that he must, finally puts his hands on her.

He touches sweat-sheened warm smooth softness. Her shoulders, first. Then, he picks up her chin, raising her face, and pulling her away from his genitals. Her eyes are clear blue-gray, with flecks of green and teal and—he cannot tell the color of her eyes, because he also sees trails of moisture along their rim, running down one cheek in a stripe.

She gasps, because she does not want him to see this, but it does not matter, because he is now holding her up, raising her from her kneeling position, and pulling down the stretch fabric from her hips.

She is suspended before him, her body naturally stiffened yet fighting it so hard to be yielding, while the pants come down her thighs, then slip down her legs. He sees the patch of amber hair at her crotch. She feels his palms touch her shoulders, then the sides of her arms. Soon, she knows, he will part her legs and it will happen. Reality seems very sharply drawn then, the candlelight searing her eyes.

He wants to touch her now, his hands drawn to her skin, to the plush softness of her large breasts which he kneads firmly, just short of hurting her. She feels a shock of something as his palms sweep across her nipples, and it makes her alert and urgent and terrified.

She expects him to part her legs, but instead he sits forward on the edge of the Chair and parts his own legs, so that she can stand between them. His penis is standing up.

He is letting her take time, she understands, and is grateful.

She draws forward, feeling his hard tip against her stomach, then puts her hands to lower it, and rises so that he can enter with more ease. "Oh Day God," she prays in her mind, then parts her own legs and there is a numbness there, and a terror, and a powerless fear of heights.

"Oh Day God," she prays, and she forces the moist insides to part further, and then starts to slide against him, slowly letting him in. . . .

He thrusts into her before she expects it, and she is at last impaled.

A gasp. He is holding her from the back by the hips. And they are both stilled, frozen in this moment of time.

He should be moving now, back and forth like a pendulum.

Instead, he is the King of Stopped Clocks.

And the blood, there below, is leaving him.

As though they both realize it then, they are suddenly thrusting, filled with urgency born of desperation and not desire.

They struggle, flesh against flesh, sliding back and forth. She rotates her hips, realizing there is a rhythm here to be followed, but the cold fire inside her—the numbness of brief arousal—has turned to pain, and she is now laboring against it, feeling his thick member inside her, hoping that his virile seed is flowing even now, as they move. But she is not sure.

Moments elongate and distend into futile infinity.

Finally he withdraws from her, limp and slick.

She immediately proceeds to do what all the other Queens before her had done. She gets up quickly and runs to the nearest wall, soft and upholstered also just for this. And she does an acrobatic move, landing into a practiced limber handstand.

He watches her in sad amusement as she stands on her hands against the wall, her hair sweeping the carpet in a gleaming pile, her feet high overhead with heels resting against the wall, her womb upright now, above her shoulders.

She is enacting a turned hourglass, hoping that the sperm will run down inside, down from the lips of her vagina and into the receptacle of the womb, giving germination a viable chance.

It is a bizarre and useless thing under any circumstances.

In that moment he grieves for her, with the complete silent sympathy and despair.

She does not fully realize he has not performed his part—or maybe she does.

However she performs hers, stubborn and determined.

She is the Queen of the Hourglass.

— 4 —

The Hourglass

Liaei hid in her room. There, in the darkness, she lay shaking, long into the night. Her mental state was hard to put into words, a combination of numb exhaustion, distress, and uncertainty.

Images layered one upon another . . . blinding candlelight, her hands anointing him, sharp intensity in her lungs with each drawn breath, focused concentration on something, distended movement. She knew that whatever had happened during the Ceremony was not exactly what should have happened; something went amiss.

The nerve endings of her body rang from the intimate contact. There was a clamor of something under the skin, and a numb soreness between her legs, wistful sorrow of confused flesh.

Something was amiss.

She knew it, because she had seen the moment of guilt followed by detachment in his eyes, a blue speck. The Clock King had been looking at her, watching her with eyes that held in them the fullness of time. Their faces had been up close, and she had a chance to observe him in turn and recognize a man of the same species as herself.

And yet, he was not quite.

The Clock King, she realized only now—in that same moment as the sobs finally broke through and she was stifling herself, burying her face into her pillow—he was a being all alone.

He had sat still in his Chair when she finally left the room. He had been silent and motionless, and seemed to have retreated back into a kind of natural stasis.

And so she slipped away from him, from that terrifying place of candlelight.

Tomorrow the barrage of fertility tests would commence, they would work on her in the City labs, and Vioma will ask questions. Liaei did not know how she would answer them.

Morning came, and instead there was only a subdued breakfast service as someone brought warm food to a room where she arrived as instructed. A table was laid out for two.

There was no sign of Vioma or anyone from the Edge City medicineal cadre. Instead, the Clock King was there.

Liaei entered, then paused, seeing him. Almost, she started to turn around but overcame herself with a force of duty.

He stood with his back to her, looking over the tall balcony window. He was dressed in ordinary clothes, a pair of jeans and simple shirt. Liaei realized this was the first time she had seen him fully clothed. She wondered what he thought of her own ordinary pull-on pants and shirt with an old spot rubbed into the fabric.

It also occurred to her that this was the first time she saw anyone living, other than herself, with a full head of hair, from the back. She watched the back of his head with a kind of intense attention, observing the growth pattern of his longish hair, how it lay over the contours of his scalp.

He turned around then, sensing her presence.

"Good morning, uhm . . . Clock King," she mumbled.

His expression as he was watching the outside view had been blank. But now, seeing her, a sort of focus, a sympathy came to the surface.

She had no means of guessing how old this man—this being—was. He seemed middle-aged, possibly young in the relative sense of the male homo sapiens of his time—what was his time?—and yet, she knew full well he was ageless, possibly thousands of years old in actual chronological years.

"Good morning, Liaei," he replied, then added, "Queen of the Hourglass."

His voice—how peculiar it was and how deep. She knew its development was due to the levels of male hormones in his body. She remembered in snatches the voices of the male singers on the ancient musical recordings she'd heard. But this was real and now.

His voice.

"That woman," he said. "Your chief nurse. Vioma? She was here earlier. She asked me to spend some time with you."

"Oh," Liaei said. "Did she ask about—"

"No."

Liaei nodded, then came to the table and poured herself a cup of hot brewed tea and took a sweet pastry.

"You never mentioned your name," she said, taking an awkward bite. "Seems weird to call you Clock King. Whatever does that mean anyway?"

In reply, he smiled, and came to the table also. He sat down, and picked up a half-full cup of his own.

"Strange, yes. But I don't know my name. I probably had one at some point. So, call me what you like."

His tone was gentle and apathetic. Just hearing him speak made her tired.

"All right, then let me think up a name for you."

Eyes the color of smoke met hers in silence.

And Liaei wondered if she need bother.

In the afternoon they strolled along a terrace overhanging the large public square of the Palace. Here on the wide open vista of the surface, the Day God filled all of the open sky except for the farthest edges and the air was dry and still with ripples of daytime heat.

The Clock King took slow steps and often lifted his hand to shield his eyes with his palm as he looked around. "So hot and bright," he said. "Your sun is fading but in the process it takes up more space and makes the whole sky appear to burn."

"You mean the Day God?" Liaei said.

"Why do you call it that?"

"What else would you call the original source of all life on earth?" she said.

"So then, it is your religion, the worship of the sun?"

Liaei crinkled up her face and then snorted. "What do you mean, worship in the historical ignorant sense? Or in the sense of never taking it for granted and seeing it as a source of energy, and even succor and inspiration? Unlike the billions of other stars, other suns out there, the Day God is ours. It sets the scale of our lives and the rhythm."

He shrugged. "An interesting definition of deity. I hope this notion stays with me the next time I am . . . brought awake."

She suddenly took his hand in hers, and tugged at it. Startled, he stopped walking. He stood before her, only slightly taller than she.

"Tell me," said Liaei, staring into his eyes. "What kinds of things have you seen? I know you have seen wonders. . . ."

"Wonders? You might say so. I've seen world wars and singularities collapsing civilizations repeatedly; entrepreneural chaos and desperate comedy and true love. I've seen a young sun that was angry-white and small and round and took up only a small spot of the blue sky. I've seen waters fill not just the whole of the Pacific Basin, but the whole world and watched them fade, until they stood only halfway up the Basin walls. And now I see this, the wonder of a sun that spans the sky."

"Who are you?" she whispered, still grasping his fingers. "No, really, who are you?"

"A man," said the Clock King. "Just a man who can never look back, only forward. It is all I can remember about myself."

"But why?" she said. "Why are you . . . *you?*"

"And why are you letting them do this to you?" he countered.

Liaei released his hand.

"Because this is all I *can* do. I was born for this, and I fit the function. And because I can, it is my duty to do so."

"But you always have a choice," he said. "You can do anything you want, and you can tell them no, and you can live your life any way you like. Even right this moment. You can just walk away from me, from this place. I, on the other hand—"

"What?" she said harshly. "You what?"

"I am . . . the Clock King."

"But that is not an answer. You have not answered my question."

The Clock King looked at her with amused sorrow. "You must ask a kind of question that I can answer. My mind does not seem to be fully my own."

The wind blew heat at them, and the filaments of their hair stood up, twisting, getting into their faces.

"I see . . ." said Liaei. "So then, there are questions that you might answer and others that you might not? You sound just like the harmonium. I ask it some things and it tells me, 'This is not a correct question.' Stupid literal thing." She snorted. And then she again took his hand, and she said, "What *is* the harmonium? Do you know? Can you tell me anything?"

He started to walk again, and she moved at his side, holding him by the arm as though he were an old man—which he was.

"Harmonium technology is based on the smallest moving parts known to humankind," he said. "It is sub-atomic, and invisible to the eye, able to switch quantum states from particle to wave. Unlike original artificial intelligence machines that were visualized to progressively mimic human intelligence, and take on a life of their own, harmonium tech created such perfectly task-compliant machines that they were deemed to be absolutely function-static. In other words, they were bound within limits of function and at the same time completely self-reliant, self-repairing, and perfectly indestructible. Like . . . clockwork."

"Okay, but what is the energy source? What makes the harmonium work?" Liaei said. "I have a feeling it is something important for me to know. Something terribly vital, a missing link. . . ."

He smiled suddenly. "You are so alive, you know that? Your own energy source is wonderful to witness. . . ."

"No, really," said Liaei. "Please, tell me!"

"Very simple. It is the energy that comes from the fluctuation between the states. Between particle and wave. Between on and off. Between existence and non-existence, life and death, love and hate—any opposites."

"So then . . . the harmonium is powered by forces of change?"

"Yes, movement, to be precise. Transition. But, why don't I show you, instead?"

Liaei stared hard at him, her thoughts in turmoil, when the man standing next to her glanced around them suddenly, looking for a familiar landmark in the air.

"There," he said, pointing to a flash of transparent molten dayfire suspended in the air. "You call it The River That Flows Through The Air."

"Oh, Day God, yes!" exclaimed Liaei. "You know it! I mean, you know what makes it behave the way it does?"

Her speech gained an urgency. "Clock King," she said, and the pressure of her fingers bit into his. "It has been obsessing me for the greater part of my life! We know—that is, our modern science knows—or at least has a good idea of many things, if not the underlying principles of the harmonium. But this impossible, inexplicable River phenomenon is still just beyond us! They are guessing that the high-tech civilization that created the harmonium level technology, disappeared—possibly to the stars—and now we have these functional harmonium systems that rely on no known power source, generate minor static fields upon occasion, and yet are able to respond to us in vocal harmonics, and readily interpret some of our commands. They are mostly unfathomable, alien things that are somehow a common part of our lives. Harmonium powers everything, or rather converts everything, and yet what makes the River flow uphill? What keeps it suspended?"

He interrupted her flow of words with a gentle touch in return, so that they were now facing each other, once again stopped.

"You think I am insane, don't you?" said Liaei suddenly. "That I am crazy? Instead of asking you prying personal questions about your own life, or just letting you be, I am trying to get a science lesson!"

"You are excited by the chance," he said. "And it appears we have stumbled upon the one thing that you really care about in your life—this River."

Liaei frowned. "I care about a great deal. About my world and these human beings who need me, about Amhama. About—"

"I know," he said. "But you care about *knowing* even more. It is natural, since just like me you are a stranger here. But to learn you need to learn how to ask."

"All right," she said. "I already know that we learn new things about harmonium technology constantly, by asking the correct type of leading questions. The harmonium is so infinitely complex that even our questions are often too basic for it. True harmonium breakthroughs are rare and momentous occasions for modern science."

"You are on the right track," he said.

"So then stop making me crazy, damn you, and just tell me!"

But the Clock King shook his head. "Not yet," he said.

Liaei was furious. She hated him then, his smug alien face with pronounced masculine features, his ageless watery eyes, his passive gentleness—what was wrong with him anyway, was he not supposed to have the same virile energy as she? She hated the way his hair tendrils curled in the heat, and how the sweat beaded along the edges of his hairline. But mostly she hated that he knew and she did not. He was withholding it from her now, just as he withheld—

"Liaei," said the most hateful man in the world. "I am to spend this time with you, and we might as well look at the world together briefly, and just observe. So then, why don't we look at The River That Flows Through The Air? How would you like to follow it as far as it flows and see what is there?"

"Absolutely not!" said Vioma in a high voice that was very unlike her, or maybe Liaei just didn't know all sides of Vioma yet. "The River flows beyond Edge City, and right into the barren desert. We are talking kilometers with hardly a road, and no one knows for how long! How can I allow this, when the two of you are supposed to be building intimacy? What if something happens to either one of you? Until you conceive, Liaei—yes, don't make embarrassed faces at me, you know perfectly well what needs be done—"

They were in Vioma's small office in the Palace lower floor. Vioma was pacing while Liaei was seated very primly on the edge of the visitor chair before the nurse's desk.

"It was the Clock King's own idea," said Liaei, looking ahead of her at the cream-colored wall and the decorative harmonium display field. "I agree with him that the two of us should go. What better way of cementing intimacy than to be alone with him on this journey? You can send some mechanical techs to watch out for us, if you like."

Vioma sighed. She stopped pacing and stood looking at Liaei, in thought. "I don't know if you're aware of this fact, Liaei, but the Clock King has only a limited amount of time here, with you. In fact, there are only a couple of days, three at most, that I can allow him to remain here with us. . . ."

Liaei stared. "What do you mean?"

"You have to conceive soon—tonight, tomorrow. And even if you do not, he still has to go back into the device. He cannot stay in this phase of existence, in our time, or he will begin accelerated atomic decay. Several times a day I monitor him—the room he is in has special bio-equipment—and he is still fine for the moment, but the decay is imminent. Left unchecked, his body will rapidly deteriorate, age and collapse. We don't know how but that ancient harmonium thing—the device—is what gives him cohesion."

"So, put him back in the device to—to recharge and take him out again in a couple of days?"

Vioma gave a rueful laugh. "It will take several decades before the chrono-mechanism will allow that. It's been timed perfectly, so that he can only be brought out to service sufficiently distinct generations."

"I see . . ." Liaei said in a dead voice.

"**O**fficer Ginadi? Are you still in Edge City?" Liaei said in a quiet but definitely living voice, using a public harmonium voice comm in the voidroom on the third floor of the Palace.

"This is Officer Ginadi," a familiar calm voice replied and Liaei heard the babble voices and sounds of a police station in the background.

"Officer, I am about to walk up a very steep slope, and I need your help."

"Liaei! Hey, is that you, kid? I mean, Queen of the Hourglass—what's wrong?"

"Yes," she said, smiling even though he could not see her since this was a basic voice link only.

"Remember the River? If you would like to see where it ends, I'd love to take a ride in your cruiser again. That is, if you don't mind two passengers."

"This is definitely going to cost me some demerits from the Committee," Ginadi was saying the next morning as he elevated the cruiser to the precise city limits hover altitude. In the back seat were the Clock King and the Queen of the Hourglass.

"Don't worry," said Liaei, decisive and serious. "I've convinced Vioma that if we don't find the River's end by the end of the day, we head back immediately."

"That woman is a harpy," said the Clock King, also very serious, and yet there was something new in his expression. "A loving one, but a harpy nevertheless."

"A what?" said Liaei.

"I have no idea," he replied. "Things I have known at other times often randomly come to mind. Terms, images, ideas, junk. All prompted to recall by a detail, by something or other in the here and now. It's good to be . . . alive."

"Clock King, you are a funny one," said Ginadi, as they started along the main street that ran by the tall support aqueduct rings of the River. "I expected you to be, well, different."

In the back seat, the Clock King smiled. "I *am* different every time," he said.

They moved rapidly through Edge City, past apartment buildings and shopping areas, and Liaei threw occasional glances behind her at the tall needle-tower of the Palace, still visible. The Day God sky was a searing bright abyss overhead, and the surrounding streets were all alike, pavement surfaces well maintained, building fronts sporting mirror-glass and harmonium displays everywhere.

"What if one day," said the Clock King all of a sudden, "the harmonium stops working? All energy just dies out? What will you do?"

"Oh, Day God, don't say that," whispered Liaei. She remembered a conversation that now seemed many years ago, Riveli speaking with her and Amhama in Basin City, saying that several transports had failed.

"I know," said the Clock King with his former apathetic tone of voice. "Your society will fall apart and you all immediately become civilized savages. And, since modern homo sapiens is born in a hothouse lab, probably using all kinds of harmonium equipment and methods, then your crisis would be severe indeed. Unless you can use other means, you are faced with total extinction within one generation."

"You certainly know how to cheer someone," said Ginadi. They were driving in a remote city area, past huge complexes of hothouse fields under plasti-glassoid cover. Here the River was flowing at a much lower altitude, a mere ten feet in the air, and frequent, narrow siphoning pipes were connected to it at the junction of the support rings. They drew the water from it by means of simple suction, to irrigate the hothouses.

"Look at all that food being grown," said the Clock King. "None of it can survive the conditions outside. Yet when the harmonium goes, you will need to come up with new mechanical means—or a new technology altogether—to keep it alive."

"Well, the economy is straightforward," said Ginadi. "All production is short-term and to order. Nothing gets wasted— unlike the historical famines and failed harvests you ancients used to experience in the agriculture of the open air and inclement weather. Now, we grow what we need, and I am sure we can figure out a way to keep it that way, ecologically self-contained."

"Self-contained is good," the Clock King said. "But self-reliant is better. Every perfect ecosystem in a bottle like yours can be shattered. You need an imperfect system that can fight to survive in the mess of broken shards. Until it can become another perfect circle. . . ."

Liaei listened to the two of them speak, and something heavy and final was settling over her, a burden of inevitable thought.

In that moment the Clock King turned to her and pointed to the dancing stripe of River outside the cruiser window.

"So, Liaei," he said. "Here it is, and we are right alongside it. What do you see?"

"What do you mean?" Liaei squinted from the reflected Day God radiance. "I see it moving and glittering, all kinds of colors and yet transparent."

The Clock King nodded in silence, and smiled. He said nothing for a long time after.

It was noon when they left the outer reaches of Edge City. There was no guard tower here, merely a small kiosk with one police officer on duty surrounded by four glassoid walls, who nodded to them while barely looking up from his harmonium display. The last walls of concrete were behind them, empty paved lots of undeveloped city property.

The paved road continued onward, past the city limits into amber desolation. On the right of it, dancing like a streak of pure energy flew the airborne River. It swept through the aqueduct rings that receded like black sentinels into the heat horizon.

"That way," said Ginadi, "lies nothing. Nothing and the rest of the world."

"We will be fine," said Liaei. "Even if the cruiser breaks down, we've plenty of water for several days, while they come to get us."

But Ginadi was more subdued. "What about him? According to your Vioma who left me very detailed instructions, he does not have several days."

"Ah, so you know . . ." said Liaei.

The Clock King grinned. "You mean that at the stroke of midnight I become a pumpkin?"

Liaei had no understanding of his words or juxtaposition of ensuing images, but she had never seen his face like that, bared teeth, fierce, exuberant, cheeks dark with the shadow of stubble. He was coming alive indeed, she realized. The shadow man who had attempted to mate with her two days ago was someone else altogether.

Here was the real Clock King.

The cruiser was speeding forward now, much more rapidly and at a higher hover altitude. The landscape of dry bleached rocks, sand, stone, and solitary spots of stunted desert cacti that required almost no water and got exactly that—all flew by in a kaleidoscope of bland scorching light.

The River That Flows Through The Air continued also, on and on into the desert, and there was no end in sight.

Ginadi spoke nothing for many kilometers now, and Liaei was guessing that he was more disturbed than he was letting on.

"Wait," she said, breaking the silence, and looked at the man seated next to her. "You must know that the River ends, don't you? Otherwise we wouldn't be just driving off into nowhere."

"Yes," the Clock King said. "I know its end. Soon."

He was looking before them as he replied, and Liaei watched his even profile, the straight nose and brow, proportioned shape of skull. It felt odd for her not to see the uncovered head shape of someone, since his was covered by hair in the back, and so his exact shape remained a mystery.

"Good," Ginadi said. And almost he exhaled in relief.

When the afternoon deepened and the Day God was just letting go of the eastern sliver of sky, the angle perspective of the receding aqueduct rings seemed to shorten in the farthest distance. Instead of continuing to recede to a sharp point, Liaei saw it grow and turn blunt and there was a widening of the horizon just beyond it.

The cutoff point was coming to them in the distance, the dark distant shape of the last support ring.

The fiery line of the River also was seeming to fade at the end of the horizon.

The road ahead was still a strip of pavement, old and weathered, and the cruiser hover-flew over it like a metallic arrow, while the cruiser's ovoid shadow raced just underneath and slightly to the left.

Judging by the angle of the Day God, they were moving north.

"There," the Clock King said suddenly. "Look!"

Liaei was already staring so hard that for the last several long moments she forgot to blink.

The end came softly.

The paved road continued on before them, fading into the horizon. But the last thick black metal ring support was just meters ahead.

The River That Flows Through The Air continued past it, about fifteen meters forward into the air, and about ten meters above the ground. The water flew sparkling, clear, joyous, reflecting amber and persimmon light.

And then, at about fifteen meters from the last ring, the water simply faded into the air.

It did not cascade down upon the ground, did not scatter into a pressureless chaos, did not fan out and rain upon the land around it.

It simply disappeared.

As though someone took an eraser and rubbed it away from the world, dissolving its edges into the air.

"Oh Day God . . ." whispered Liaei.

Ginadi slowed the cruiser and, losing hover altitude, it came to an even stop, parking extensions gripping the pavement.

For a moment they sat motionless, watching.

Then Liaei pressed a release and the doors were unlocked and she burst outside into the scalding dry wind and rarified air. The two men followed her.

Liaei walked, tripping over small rocks that were scattered along the long unused pavement of the road, and then her footsteps slowed as she came to the place where, overhead, the sheet of water disappeared into nothing.

Liaei stretched out her hand to feel the air just below the point of *end*, expecting an invisible barrier, an energy field, a something.

There was none.

She craned her neck, standing right underneath, but did not even feel any moisture in the wind, a spray, nothing.

"What . . . in the world . . . is that?" asked Ginadi, coming to stand at her side.

Just behind them the Clock King laughed.

"Please . . ." said Liaei, turning to him. "Please explain!" The Clock King stopped laughing because he might have seen that the Queen of the Hourglass had tears in her eyes.

"What is that? Where is the water going?"

"Liaei," he said. Although he spoke quietly, he sounded sober and hard. "Remember that you have to ask the right questions, both of me and the harmonium."

Officer Ginadi folded his hands, listening.

"Yes . . ." breathed Liaei. "I remember."

"Then, think! Before you ask, consider the whole River. You have seen its full length. Tell me what you have seen."

She gripped her shirt, wringing its ends with her fingers.

"I don't know. There was . . . first there was the big canal pipe coming straight out of the refinery plant that's on the shore. We drove by it. It had those same rings around it—"

"Yes," the Clock King said. "Go on."

"Then, the Basin slope started to incline uphill, and the water pipe went with it. I have no idea how the water was behaving inside the enclosure of the pipe, but I am assuming it moved the same way it did later on up-slope, once the pipe ran out. In other words, no pressure mechanism to pump it. The support rings made sense for the pipe, holding it in place against the steep slope. But once there was no pipe, it stopped making sense. Are the support rings harmonium-based? Am I right to guess that they have some kind of effect upon the water?"

"Yes."

Liaei exclaimed. "Oh, then—then, are they generators of some kind of force fields?"

The Clock King smiled. "You are almost on the right track. Let me help you to think this through. Consider for a moment, Liaei—what did the water look like, running through the rings? I am sure you've had plenty of time to observe it as you traveled alongside it."

"It was shining. And it looked clear and transparent—"

"And?"

"Well, it was purified, we know that much. So, unlike the Oceanus water, it had no pollutants."

"What did it look like, Liaei?"

Liaei's forehead was puckering with effort.

"I already told you, it was clear and sparkling in the light—"

"What colors did you see?"

"Colors? Well, it seemed golden yellow in the light, or it seemed—"

Liaei clutched her hands together. She dwelled deep into her memory of the several days before, the monotony, the mesmerizing shadows, the prismatic flow of light. . . .

"There were blue and green shadows at times, and other colors. In fact, I saw all kinds of colors in it."

"Good! And did you notice any pattern about the occurrence of colors, from the point where the water first emerged from the pipe, up till now?"

"I think there were maybe more green and blue shadows when it first emerged halfway up the slope? While here near the end it seems perfectly clear . . ."

"Yes!" the Clock King said. "Then you did see it, Liaei! Yes!"

"What did I see?" she said, frowning. "I am confused!"

"Liaei, think! Clean water is transparent, and darker water, the kind that seems to contain colors in it, indicates it contains some other particles, possibly pollutants. So, how can that be? You are saying the refinery plant pumps clean water into the canal, so then unless the pipe is dirty or contaminated, is should be perfectly transparent as it emerges and stay that way all along."

"That pipe is not dirty," put in Ginadi. "We do regular non-intrusive molecular tests every two years along random checkpoints, and it is near-sterile on the inside."

"So then," the Clock King said, "somehow the River water emerges from the unknown conditions of the pipe with acquired pollutants, and then gradually loses them as it moves along the length of its course until it is perfectly clear, yes?"

"Yes, but I don't understand!" Liaei said.

"And," continued the Clock King, "it also moves uphill against the force of earth's gravity, without any known mechanical means. Finally, it seems to be suspended in the air. Three unexplained phenomena. Can you put the three together and come up with the right question?"

They stood through long moments of silence. Wind blew at them, scalding.

"Think outside of everything, Liaei!" said the Clock King suddenly, wildly. "Think beyond and outside the limits and think the most insane impossibilities!"

Liaei raised an intense face to look at him silently.

"When?" she said. "*When* does the River flow?"

The Clock King seemed to let out a great breath of relief. "That's the question!"

He spoke, then suddenly moved forward and took her by the shoulders and pulled her into an embrace. "You can think, yes you can think, my Queen of the Hourglass. . . . All will be well now," he muttered softly into her hair, stroking the back of her head.

They were back inside the cruiser, turned around and driving home toward Edge City.

"To be precise, the River actually does not flow through space at all," the Clock King was continuing his explanation. "It simply *exists* along a near infinite range of temporal phases throughout the course of the past several million years. What you see is the water at the different levels of the great earth ocean all along the rising incline of the Basin slope, as it had been when the waters stood high, low, and all places in-between, and with various levels of salt and chemical content. Also, there is no force of uphill gravity to contend with, because the containment rings select and keep the 'cross-section' of water in that other place and time."

"So, then," said Liaei, "as far as the water is concerned, it is supported by many cubic tons of other water underneath it—in another time. And the containment rings define and focus the time field boundaries."

"Exactly. It's never flowing through the air but existing at a time when there was other water there to support it underneath. Where there is now air, used to be a great universal ocean. Indeed, when the ancient polar snow caps melted, water levels rose to cover all the surface of the earth. It receded eventually, due to global warming and greenhouse effects that broke down the protective atmospheric layers and allowed evaporation into space. Indeed, it receded several times, and yet the ingenious scientists of those epochs managed to bring it back. They did it many times, in fact. Only with the advent of the harmonium civilization did homo sapiens finally figure out the best way to keep water indefinitely on this planet, to hold on to it—by recycling it in time."

Ginadi shook his head, in sincere amazement.

"But why the canal pipe?" Liaei asked. "Why bother building it at all when the time field rings were there already, going all the way to the bottom of the Basin?"

"Not sure," the Clock King said. "But it seems to me that the canal pipe was not built by the harmonium civilization at all, but was an ignorant, unnecessary retrofit by some less knowledgeable and more recent civilization."

"There is one other question left," Liaei mused. "What happens to the River in the very end? *When* does it go?"

"Again, think about the overall pattern, Liaei. With the last support ring, the range of the temporal field is dissipated, but the water has to go somewhere. Since the water starts at the most recent time phase at the bottom of the Basin, here at the end of its course it's most likely that it goes farther and farther into the depths of history, to the very beginning. To the time when the planet was young and the oceans were newly forming. I would not be surprised—knowing the harmonium's reliance upon single perfectly circular function—if this water in fact "seeds" our planet in the first place."

Liaei had a faraway expression on her face. "Somewhere in prehistory, a strange mysterious waterfall is pouring cubic tons of water seemingly from out of the thin air, and the water is pooling around and moving out. . . ."

"Why not? Like the Clock, like the Hourglass, like any other chronometric device, time is an endless circle," the Clock King said.

She never did conceive. Liaei was tested in the Edge City medicineal, and the remaining two days she spent with the Clock King, but they were engaged in mental intimacy. They did not touch again, but sat across from each other, or walked together, and talked with all the voices they had, deep into the nights.

Vioma and other Committee members were upset and unhappy with the course of events, but they would never coerce. Personal coercion of any kind was not legal in the here and now, and so they had to make do with hoping and waiting, and attempts at persuasion.

"You remember nothing at all of your life before this strange confinement? What happens to you when you are inside the Clock device?" asked Liaei as the two of them spent the last evening together.

"Nothing. I remember only the loss of consciousness. Each time I regain awareness, I am in a new world, and a new hopeful Queen of the Hourglass with her new agenda greets me."

"How many?" Liaei said softly. "How many Queens had there been?"

He glanced into the cup he held in his hands, swirling the dark warm brew. "They blur into one woman. I cannot tell you. Not because any of them are not unique and memorable in their own way, but because in the performing of their function they necessarily lose the self and became the function. Except for you—"

Liaei listened.

"You are the first to be more concerned with how the function fits within the overall greater framework of the world. You are so eager and ready to think outside the apparent limits."

"Maybe because it seems to me that the future of our species depends more on originality of thought and eccentricity of action than on good old fashioned genetic procreative viability. You gave me that much—oh, Clock King, I could never express how much you opened me! All my life was for this. And I expected some kind of resigned inevitable outcome— a pregnancy, the child, the rest of our pre-planned lives, constant medic intrusion, frustrated loneliness for both of us. And now, oh Day God, I don't know anything anymore! And it is so liberating! If we all die as a species tomorrow—which we will not—even so, it is now a fresh clean vista of possibility. Not fertile genes but a fertile mind."

He got up and since it was still light outside, suggested they take a walk. He was fierce with eagerness to see, once they had come outside on the Palace terraces.

"I keep on thinking what else is different," the Clock King said, looking up at the blazing sky, "and now it occurs to me. There are no birds. Nothing living flying overhead. No insects."

"All extinct," said Liaei in a quiet voice. "The horticulturists have some of the old species' DNA in storage, and in theory they could bring to term and harvest avian or insect beings. Only, why should they? With such frugal distribution of resources, it is senseless and irresponsible—at least in the here and now."

"You are Gods," he said. "Really, you are. In the way you make such decisions."

"Isn't every complex organism a God compared to a less complex one? Well, maybe not, I suppose—not unless they are capable of the function of creation."

He nodded.

"And you are the Clock King. What exactly do you rule? I am sorry to be blunt, but it seems to me that you are the one ruled by the whim of others, by this harmonium device, and by time itself."

The Clock King nodded again. "That is exactly so. What I rule is one thing only. Not myself but my function—as do you."

Liaei moved long strands of hair out of her face. "I don't know," she said. "Now I think I rule nothing at all, and I am not really the Queen of the Hourglass."

"We can go back inside and try once more," he offered with kindness, and she knew exactly what he meant, and that he was indeed now showing her that he was ruled by and ruling in turn his sole function, which required the activation of hers.

But she was not fooled.

"No," she replied, taking his hand. "It would be best that we left it at that."

Intense dark eyes were looking into hers.

"You will be alone for the rest of your life, Liaei," he said. "After I am gone, there may not be another . . ."

"Yes, I know. But fortunately, hormonal levels diminish. Time will be my friend in this sense. There will be other ways, and other things and people to occupy me."

He smiled.

The evening went on, filled with their animated voices, long into the night. He told her of glittering seas and ships and wars and armies spreading flaming destruction, of miraculous breakthroughs of science, of religions and sacrament, of family units and bonds, of the arts and human achievement, of languages and the different forms of writing used by the ancients to symbolically record speech, of other species of animals and of green plants that once grew freely on the surface of the planet, of civilizations falling, rising, and going to the stars. . . .

In the morning, it was time for him to go.

There was no ceremony this time. Vioma, several medic techs, and Liaei, accompanied the Clock King to the grand hall where the ancient Clock device lay gaping open, ready to swallow him up again and sweep him forward in time.

The Clock King had shaved and cleansed himself and was once more smooth and naked and ever-so vulnerable to time and atomic decay and all of the world. But his eyes were wild and glittering with bright moisture, more alive than they had ever been. Just before entering the device chamber he turned to Liaei, took her face between his hands, and kissed her on the lips.

His mouth was cool and gentle and kind. "It's been a time. Remember to always ask the right question, Queen of the Hourglass . . ." he whispered, for her ears only. And then he turned his gaze away from her and stepped within the Clock.

As the techs initiated the lock sequence, Liaei stood rooted to the spot and motionless and numb with loss. With a rising hum the face of the Clock lifted and covered his form, and his eyes were already staring vacant into eternity.

But Liaei was not deceived.

The Clock King was ruling his function, but he had been the one who showed her how to grow beyond hers.

And because he did thus, because she now visualized so many options, Liaei knew that one day it may no longer be necessary to awaken the Clock King ever again. Thus, insidiously he freed himself.

She only hoped that by then the circle of time swept him forward sufficiently that none of this any longer mattered.

Whatever that meant.

Liaei listened to the hum and the ticking, watched the many hands of the Clock rotating and aligning. And when the particular sequence was over and silence returned, she followed Vioma to the medicineal for the last sequence of tests.

They may be hopeful still, and she owed them that much, but she knew full well that she was already free.

Later in the day she would request they give her access to the old harmonium files, the records kept of the Clock King. She would read them in silence as she learned the act of letting go.

“I missed you, Ama!” Liaei said over the voice comm in her room at the Palace. On the other end, somewhere far down in Basin City, her foster parent’s gentle timbre sounded as intimate and dear as anything Liaei ever imagined.

“Yes, it has been wonderful and incredible,” Liaei continued. “But unfortunately I did not manage to become pregnant. Yes, he is gone now, and I miss him in a strange way. I miss his mind. And yet, Ama, I miss you even more. The things he told me and taught me, they are even more wonderful and important in retrospect! I am going to study some more on my own and work on the harmonium and think. And I will stay here in Edge City just a while longer.”

After their conversation ended, Liaei stood up, and stretched, and called for music, and danced in the privacy of her self, to the rhythms of the ancients. She shut her eyes and pretended he spun with her, his olive-skinned hands touching hers lightly in a remote circle of an embrace.

There was so much to do, to learn, to try. So many questions to ask. There was The River That Flows Through The Air, and she had to visit its end-place one more time and look and think.

Liaei danced, hands outflung, spinning and moving, her hair fanning with the circular motion.

At one point she noticed the gift box from Toliwe and Finnei, still unopened, still lying on top of her things on the cabinet. "Open it when you are bored," they had told her.

I will never be bored, thought Liaei, and took the box and opened it anyway, not in curiosity, but to test herself, because she knew exactly what would be inside.

Wrapped in fine shimmering fabric lay a pendant on a chain, a replica of an antique hourglass, with two glassoid compartments, one of them filled with granules of some shining bluish substance.

"Yes," said Liaei to herself. "That was exactly what I thought it would be. But it no longer applies."

She wondered now, what were those bluish granules, those substitutes for real sand.

Because out there, many kilometers beyond Edge City, it lay, sand and dust. And the River flew in the air, and alongside it ran the old paved road. And after the River faded out of sight, the road still continued.

Liaei was going to find out where the road ended, even if it meant following it past the horizon.

But for now, she simply flipped over the hourglass, observing the falling grains, the simple mystery and beauty of its self-contained circular motion.

So easy to simply break the glass. . . .

The curious difficulty would be to preserve the hourglass whole and yet manage to learn what is inside, merely by observing its function.

In her mind's eye, hurtling through time, the Clock King laughed.

ABOUT THE AUTHOR

Vera Nazarian immigrated to the USA from the former USSR as a kid, sold her first story at the age of 17, and since then has published numerous works in anthologies and magazines, and has seen her fiction translated into eight languages.

She made her novelist debut with the critically acclaimed arabesque "collage" novel *Dreams of the Compass Rose*, followed by epic fantasy about a world without color, *Lords of Rainbow*. Her novella *The Clock King and the Queen of the Hourglass* from PS Publishing with an introduction by **Charles de Lint** made the *Locus* Recommended Reading List for 2005. Her debut short fiction collection *Salt of the Air*, with an introduction by **Gene Wolfe**, contains the 2007 Nebula Award-nominated "The Story of Love." Recent work includes the 2008 Nebula Award-nominated, self-illustrated baroque fantasy novella *The Duke In His Castle,* the Jane Austen parody *Mansfield Park and Mummies* (2009), and *Northanger Abbey and Angels and Dragons* (2010).

Vera lives in Los Angeles and is working on a number of book-length projects including *Lady of Monochrome,* a sequel to *Lords of Rainbow,* a new Compass Rose milieu novel *Gods of the Compass Rose,* the *Airealm* trilogy, and medieval-gothic *Cobweb Bride.* She uses her Armenian sense of humor and her Russian sense of suffering to bake conflicted pirozhki and make art.

In addition to being a writer and award-winning artist, she is also the publisher of Norilana Books.

Official website:
www.veranazarian.com

Publication Credits

"What is Time?" **American Poetry Anthology,** Volume I, Number 3-4, edited by John Frost, Fall/Winter 1982.

"The Ballad of Universal Jack," **New Writings in the Fantastic,** edited by John Grant, Pendragon Press, UK, September 2007.

"A Time to Crawl," ***Bookface.com,*** July 2000.

"Faces at the End of Time," **Beyond the Last Star:** *Stories from the Next Beginning,* edited by Sherwood Smith, SFF Net, August 2002.

"Port Custodial Blues," *Helix #2,* edited by William Sanders and Lawrence Watt-Evans, October 2006. (WSFA Small Press Award 2007 Finalist.)

"The Ice," *Colonies #3,* edited by John Dunne, Regent Publications, UK, 2000.

"Mount Dragon," *Talebones,* Issue #14, Winter (January) 1999.

"Salmon in the Drain Pipe," original to this collection.

"Scent of the Stars," original to this collection.

The Clock King and the Queen of the Hourglass, introduction by Charles de Lint, PS Publishing, UK, October 2005.

www.ingramcontent.com/pod-product-compliance
Lightning Source LLC
Chambersburg PA
CBHW030519020726
47494CB00004B/1151